I0575385

JUMPER

Karma Police Book One

SEAN PLATT

DAVID W. WRIGHT

STERLING & STONE

JUMPER

Chapter One

SATURDAY

≈

THREE HUNDRED FIFTY-SIX.

I wake up remembering the number as if it's the most important thing in the world. As far as I'm concerned, it is.

Today is the 356th day that I've woken in a body that wasn't my own. Three hundred and fifty-six days since I've been myself — a self I no longer remember.

Today, I wake as a woman named Lara Spencer. Her other details must still be coming, like an old computer starting up, preparing files for me to access. First are the immediate things: the location of Lara's buzzing alarm so my hand can reach out and find the clock without fumbling; figuring out if I'm alone in bed (I am); and then the detail that usually dictates how difficult this occupation will be — whether my host lives alone.

It's infinitely easier to wake up as someone living by themselves, rather than a person who lives with friends or

1

family. Living with others, I have to be instantly on guard, second-guessing my every instinct, wondering if my actions are something my host for the day (or days) would do. Or worse, if my actions will somehow reveal the truth — that I am not the person they think I am.

That's the most frustrating part of all this — I call it *jumping*, from body to body — not remembering who I, *The Jumper*, am. I can barely remember details of all but the most recent lives I've been living. Everything else is a blur of memories, none of which, to my knowledge, belong to *me*.

I only remember the number.

It's the last thing I do before I go to sleep each night. I add one to that day's total, so I wake up remembering how many days I've been on this journey. It's my markings on the prison wall of a sentence served separated from my body. That number is the only anchor to my life before this.

Even the number could be a lie, though, as the only thing I have to go on is my fuzzy memories.

The first body I remember waking up in that wasn't my own was that of a man named Scott Cooper. He'd been in a car accident and was in a coma. I thought I *was* Scott — that it was *me* in a vegetative state, and this was my new reality. I could hear the nurses and his wife talking to him. It was sheer hell to feel barred from all response, attempting to will his body to move, to speak, to do *something!* I figured I'd found myself in a real-life purgatory, but then I woke the next day as a woman named Valerie and realized that something else was happening to me.

Since then I wake up, usually every day, sometimes every couple of days, as somebody else. I've been both sexes, children and seniors, and held occupations from cop to criminal. I've yet to find any rhyme, reason, or common thread among my hosts save for one: they all live on or near the West Coast. Sometimes, I've woken a few states inland, but generally speaking that's the only common denominator.

But it isn't enough to suss out how or why this is happening to me.

Or who I am.

It is said that we are the sum of our experiences. But my experiences of the past year are not my identity. They belong to others, borrowed by me. And if I am not the sum of stolen experiences, then what am I?

Who am I?

Each day I feel like the answer is on the tip of my tongue if only I can piece some unseen puzzle together.

The alarm's annoying bray shatters any attempt at thinking through this.

As my hand finds the button to kill the alarm, I look at the time.

7:14 a.m.

I sit up in bed as details of my host bleed into my brain. I'm twenty-four, a college grad working as a graphic designer at an online paper called the *Bay Cove Chronicle* — Clay County, Washington's Finest News Source, as they say. I look around the bedroom. Violet walls lined with photos, drawings, and paintings. I'm not sure how many, if any, of these are Lara's work. I could try and search her memories for some background, but it's probably not worth the hassle. The more I probe my host's memories, the worse the headaches inside their bodies. I'm not sure why this is, though I have a theory that there is some part of the host person still here. But I have no way of knowing for certain, and every attempt to engage the person inside results in me talking to myself.

It's best to let memories come as needed. And that's

how they most often arrive: on a need-to-know basis. I'll usually get a sliver of recall — not enough to draw context of why a particular memory is important, or how it relates to other things. Which is why this is always so much harder when I wake up in large families.

I get up and head to the shower.

The hot water beats on my scalp. I let my mind wander, hoping for something that might belong to me. But nope. Today, I'm only getting random thoughts from Lara's head, chief among them a date she's scheduled for tonight, with a guy named Gavin. They've been talking online for nearly four months, but they haven't yet met.

So, of course, the night Lara's not here will be that first date.

Damn.

I have two choices. I can go on the date or reschedule it. But as I try and sift through her memories, I can't find anything that might help me make the right decision.

This is one of the other difficult parts about this thing. I never know when I'm going to be in a host's body on an important day. And seeing as I have no idea what my host remembers when they return to their body, I don't want to shortchange them of an important memory.

I can only imagine how many relationships I have inadvertently ruined because *I* was in a person's body on an important day. My actions could alter the course of someone's entire life for better or for worse. I'd hate to think this date could be The One, and my canceling might ruin everything. On the flip side, what if we have a fantastic first date, then tomorrow, or whenever Lara returns, her evening is a mystery? That would screw things up even worse.

I've found workarounds — like getting blind-ass drunk,

enough that it would explain to anyone, including the host, why they couldn't remember anything.

But that's always a last resort, and it's rarely practical.

I always try to leave a host's life exactly the same as when I was imprisoned inside it. Which isn't always easy to do.

Too often I've found myself in the life of someone in dire need of change. A woman being verbally or physically abused by a boyfriend or husband, a worker being shit on by their boss, or someone wasting their potential with horrible choices or a general lack of action.

I want to shake the host's body, and yell at them, "What the hell are you doing?" And it's so hard not to clean up their messes. Leave their shitty boyfriends, quit their jobs, get them off their asses — something to improve their lives in some way.

But I know that no matter what I do, I can't improve their lives forever. And I'm likely to mess everything up, especially if they have no recollection of events from when I was in their bodies.

I often do nothing.

I get out of the shower and get dressed. I start to pick a red shirt from Lara's closet but get a flash of something telling me that she'd never wear that shirt. I find a pair of jeans and a long-sleeved blue tee, which feels immediately better.

I step out of my bedroom, surprised to find that I'm not alone after all. Sleeping on the couch, beneath a large red throw, is a teenage girl.

I'm confused, but then a name pops into my head — Allie Martin. The fifteen-year-old who lives in an apartment down the hall.

Why is she here?

Did she spend the night at Lara's? Was Lara babysitting?

I can't find anything in Lara's memories regarding last night. I only remember fragments from yesterday's host. I'm certain that something is wrong with the girl, though I'm not sure what. I need to wake Allie and find out why she's here.

I go over, gently touch her shoulder and give a gentle shake.

She turns, groggily wiping her long brown hair from her face, then looks up at me. Confusion surrenders to a smile. "Good morning. I hope you don't mind. Mom was in bad shape last night."

I'm not sure what she means or what that has to do with her being on Lara's couch. Then I'm hit with a flash of memory: Allie crying in Lara's doorway, bruises on her left cheek and eye. Lara telling her she doesn't have to take it. She can call the sheriff's office. But Allie won't do that. Lara gives her a key to her apartment and says, "Next time she gets like this, you come here. Okay? Even if I'm not home. You come here and wait her out."

I don't know if this is the first time Allie has taken her up on the offer or the umpteenth.

I sit next to her on the couch and say, "Sorry."

I'm not sure how much affection I should show. Would Lara hug Allie to let her know things are okay? Or would she keep a comfortable distance? I don't know Allie, *or* Lara, despite wearing her body. So much for the ease of living alone.

After a moment of silence, Allie leans on me.

I'm guessing this is normal, so I don't flinch away despite feeling compelled to. It's always weird when people show affection, or any kind of intimate relationship, with my host. It feels like a stranger violating my personal space.

Like, *wait, I don't know you; why are you hugging me?* I always have to fight the urge to pull back, pretend so as not to break the illusion or offend them.

But there's something else, too.

A part of *me* that doesn't want to become attached to people I'll be leaving in a day or two.

I wrap my arm around Allie. "So, how bad was it this time?"

"She was close to getting violent again. I don't even know what set her off. I was in my room doing homework, and she just burst in, lit up, bitching about God knows what. Something to do with her work, but then what an ungrateful little bitch I am and how she should never have had me."

It hurts to hear this. I've been inside too many people who've been on the receiving end of this kind of hate, and I still can't understand it. I know the abuser is usually hurt themselves, and often a victim as well, but being a victim, you'd think they'd understand what they're doing. You'd think they wouldn't inflict such hate toward their own child. Don't they have any self-awareness, recognition of what they're doing? Can't they stop?

I suppose it's only a matter of time before I find myself inside the body of just such an abuser. Maybe I'll get a firsthand taste of *why* they do what they do. Of why they can't quit. God, I hope not. I hope that if and when it happens I'll have the self-awareness to stop. Maybe break the cycle for someone. But how can I know that any good I do in a body will have any lasting impact? Maybe I won't treat my family like shit for a day or two, but then once I'm gone, will it be a return to hell for them? A pleasant memory left behind, like a family vacation they'll never take again? Perhaps my kindness would only prolong the misery, giving a husband or wife enough false hope to ignore the decay of their rotting relationship — thinking that maybe the person is capable of kindness, that maybe they'll change if only the abused can just wait a little longer.

"So, what happened next?" I ask Allie.

"I bolted, said maybe she'd be better off if I left. She pointed at the door and laughed, 'Go. You won't last a day on your own!'"

"Don't you think she'll be worried?"

"Nah, she won't even remember when she wakes up. Whenever that is. Today's Saturday, so it probably won't be until four or five."

I shake my head.

Allie's so casual. It must happen all the time.

She looks at me, "Can I come to your office again? I really don't want to go back on the off chance she's still awake and drinking."

A burst of memories explodes in my mind, showing me Allie spending several Saturdays at the office with Lara. She's a budding artist herself, so she loves watching Lara work, even if it's on stuff that isn't especially artistic.

"Sure," I say, hoping it's okay to bring her in without calling anyone.

"Mind if I shower and change?" Allie pats a backpack on the ground.

"Sure," I say, wondering just how normal this is for the girl. A part of me wants to talk some sense into her mother. But if Lara hasn't done it before now, there must be a reason. In all likelihood, I'll only make things worse for Allie.

❧

8

As WE DRIVE to my office, Allie talks about going to college. I wonder if this is as animated as she gets. She seems reasonably sure she can get an art scholarship for a school on the East Coast and get far away from here. She just hopes she can wait out the raging storm of her mother's mood swings long enough to escape.

I wish I had advice to give her, but my childhood is a mystery. I don't even know my original name or sex. I only have the jumbled bits of the lives I've lived against my will, without the history or context to know how things worked out after I left. A part of me thinks that what Lara's doing now seems like the best course of action. Would her life be any better if she had her mother arrested, or if she was put into the foster care system? Maybe her best bet is to tolerate this life as long as she can, then run away and never look back.

But I won't tell her that. I don't want to contradict any of Lara's previous advice. Plus, she and Allie have a history. She probably has a better idea than I do how severe the abuse is. From what I know of teenagers, reality is often amplified beyond how an adult would see it. Maybe things are bad at home, without being devastating.

I feel awful for thinking this, especially with the memory of Allie's bruised face lurking in Lara's head.

Lara's phone buzzes in my purse. I'm driving, so Allie offers to see who it is.

"It's Yvonne. She wants you to pick up her regular from Starbucks."

I draw a blank, then Lara's memories fill me in. Latin woman, mid-thirties, editor at the online newspaper. Her regular is an iced coffee, two sugars, extra cream.

"Tell her okay," I say, accessing Lara's memories to find the closest Starbucks. Memories are interesting in the way they *usually* fill me in on the stuff I need to know just as I need to know it. I hope her memories continue to come forth as needed, as I don't know the first thing about graphic design. If Lara's skills refuse to kick in, I'll have to find a graceful exit.

Sometimes, a host's memories will fail me at the worst possible time. I've had to leave work more often than I care to admit, or could probably count. A few times, jobs have intimidated me so much that I had to call in sick knowing there was no way I could fake it well enough to get by. Like the time I woke up as an airline pilot. I wasn't about to take people's lives in my hands by hoping the skills would come to me. So I live by a simple rule: If I don't think I can do the job, or my attempt might endanger people or lose someone their job, I stay home. This allows me to adhere to my prime directive: *never interfere with my host's life.*

I ARRIVE at the office with coffee, and Allie, in hand.

"Hey, Allie, how's it going?" Yvonne says, directing her to one of the design room's three empty chairs.

The two girls talk with immediate comfort, suggesting that Allie accompanying Lara to the job isn't uncommon. Yvonne is either an understanding boss or the paper offers a lax work environment.

The paper is small with only six non-advertising staffers and a core group of only four people: the editor Yvonne, Lara, and two reporters named Katelynn and Tommy — neither are at the office today. The paper also has stringers and interns who do a bulk of the weekday reporting. But today is Saturday, and the paper's only residents are Yvonne and Lara, working to finish the Sunday edition.

Yvonne updates me on what needs to be finished: last-minute changes to client ads and tweaking a few story images, while she finishes editing copy.

Allie spends much of the morning surfing the web on one of the computers next to me and chatting with Yvonne, who is *very* talkative. I'm thankful for Allie. If she weren't here, I'd get nothing done, or Yvonne might notice me stumbling through some basic Photoshop work.

At one, Yvonne asks us to join her for lunch at the corner diner.

WE'RE SQUEEZED into a cozy booth in the back, waiting for our food. "So, tonight's the big night, eh?" Yvonne says.

I play dumb, not sure if Lara had told Yvonne about the date or if she's talking about something else. I don't want to reveal something Lara wouldn't want to be known.

Yvonne looks at me grinning. "Oh, come on, don't act like you're not excited."

"Oh, you're finally meeting *Gavin?*" Allie asks with a wide smile that seems older than her age. "Why didn't you tell me?"

"I dunno," I say. Is this the sort of stuff that Lara would share with Allie? It must be since she knew his name.

"How long have you been talking to him?" Yvonne asks.

"Four months," I say like it's no big deal.

"Show me the pic again."

I draw a blank.

She grabs my phone from the table and starts thumbing through the screen. I guess Yvonne and Lara have that kind of relationship where such intrusions are normal. Allie, sitting beside me, is cracking up.

I let Yvonne thumb through the photos on Lara's phone. She finds one of a young blond-haired man in a tight white T-shirt, lean muscles rippling under the surface. The photo looks like it's ripped from an Abercrombie & Fitch catalog.

Yvonne says, "I am soooo jealous."

"Jealous? You've got Tony," I say, suddenly remembering her boyfriend's name.

"Yeah, but Tony doesn't look like *this!* I'm telling you, this shit's not fair. You haven't put in enough time on the dating circuit to get a guy like this. How many boyfriends have you had?"

"I don't know," I answer honestly.

"Three in your whole life. At least that's what you told me. You know how many men I had to date before I found Tony?"

Allie's laughing hard. "You've only had three boyfriends?"

"Three isn't bad," I say, suddenly feeling like a prude. "And besides, the last one was awful. It was like having four boyfriends, all of them jerks."

"But you're so old," Allie says, "I thought you would've had more by now."

"Old? I'm twenty-four!"

Yvonne looks at Allie with a faux glare. "Watch it now, girl. 'Cuz Lara's the young one at the paper."

"I'm sorry." Allie covers her laugh. "I'm just saying that most people have had more than three boyfriends by the time they're out of high school."

"How many have you had?" I ask, a bit too defensively.

Allie looks like I hurt her feelings for a moment but quickly recovers. "You know my mom won't let me date. Plus, the last thing in the world I wanna do is get knocked up in school and have a child I hate like she does."

That chills the mood.

Thankfully, the food comes a minute later to occupy our mouths.

After a bit, Yvonne says, "It's okay. I'm sure you'll have boys beating down your door once you get to college."

"You think?" Allie asks.

"Oh, I know. You're way too pretty. But don't go falling for the first smile you see. Hold out, and maybe you'll land yourself a *Gavin.*"

We all laugh, the mood lightened.

Yvonne says, "Well if it doesn't work out, you can always ask Tommy out."

Tommy is a reporter at the paper. I'm not sure of the history between Lara and Tommy, so I let the comment go, and change the subject. "Nope, if this doesn't work, I'm giving up on guys. I'll just settle down with a house full of cats or something."

"No," Yvonne laughs, sliding the phone back to me. "I've got a good feeling about this."

I try to cover my anxiety, but Yvonne sees through it.

"It's gonna be okay, girl."

"Yeah," Allie says with a mouthful of fries.

"I dunno. A part of me wants to call the whole thing off, stay home, pig out on ice cream while binging on Netflix."

The words come from my mouth faster than intended. And this is when things can get dangerous. The longer I'm in someone, the more comfortable I feel, and the more attuned to their speech patterns I feel. So I sometimes talk too fast, before the memories have had a chance to fill themselves in, which has hurled me into some sticky conversations. For instance, Lara might not have Netflix, and Yvonne and Allie might know this. Hell, maybe Lara is an outspoken opponent of online streaming services; I don't know. But nobody seems to take exception, so the conversation rolls forward with the girls reassuring me that it's okay to be nervous, and things will be just fine.

I don't argue much.

I only know that the longer I wait to call this guy, the worse it's going to be for Lara once I leave.

I have to figure out what I'm going to do.

It feels good having friends like this. At least for today. I feel a pang of loneliness that I'll never see either of them again.

That's one of the worst things about being a Jumper — my only word for what's happening to me. I can never connect with anyone. Make my own friends. Find my own love.

I suppose some people would think I'm lucky, particularly the people I've been in who literally have no one in their lives to care about them. They would see me having thousands of friends and hundreds of loves. But none of it means anything when it's all so ephemeral. When every new body is a fresh reminder of my eternal loneliness.

Suddenly, the phone rings.

I look at the screen.

GAVIN.

My eyes must widen because Yvonne and Allie are both giving me the same expectant look.

"Get it!" Allie says, laughing.

I pick up.

"Hello?" I say, no clue how Lara typically answers his calls. I know they've talked on the phone a lot, so I'm hoping he can't sense anything off about Lara today.

"Lara?"

Does he already sense something's off?

"Yes," I say. "Gavin?"

"Yeah, how's it going?"

And just like that, my heart's racing faster. Not out of love, lust, or any of the usual suspects. No. My heart is racing because Gavin's voice sounds familiar. Not just familiar — but stop-your-heart-you-just-heard-a-ghost kind of familiar — the kind of voice you never forget.

Yet I can't remember where I've heard it. I want to think it's from another of the many bodies before Lara, but what if that's not it? What if he's from my actual life? What if he knows the real me?

"It's going okay," I say, still trying to figure out where I've heard his voice. "Just having lunch with Yvonne."

"Ah, okay. Don't wanna keep ya. Just making sure we're still on for tonight. Old House at eight?"

Lara's mind tells me that Old House is a nice restaurant downtown. She's been there once before, with Yvonne and Kenny, for Kenny's twenty-ninth birthday dinner.

"Yes, Old House at eight." My hands are clammy. I can feel sweat between my breasts, down my back. I feel like I'm choking on words.

"You okay?"

"Yeah, just excited to finally meet!" I say, trying my best to sound sincere.

And I *am* sincere. Because while I don't know much, I do know this is the first voice I've heard in a long time that holds a promise to unlocking my past.

"See you tonight," I say, scared and excited all at once.

IT'S BEEN TEN MINUTES, and my date still hasn't shown up.

The waiter walks by a few times over the next ten minutes, with this look on his face — a cross between pity and embarrassment as it becomes increasingly obvious that I'm being stood up.

I call Gavin, but it goes straight to voice mail. Not even a personalized message, but the robotic female voice telling me that the caller is unavailable, and to please leave a message.

I do, trying not to sound desperate, or anxious.

I run my finger along my glass, ice melting while I wonder what to do next. I told myself that I'd leave once my water was gone, but now I'm finishing my second glass.

I feel everyone's eyes upon me as if all the happy couples are looking at me in judgment. I tell myself that no one is looking. I've been body jumping long enough to know that most people are so absorbed in their lives, wondering if people are looking at them, that they rarely pay attention to strangers, much less show much concern for whether someone in a restaurant has been stood up.

Yet I can't shake the feeling of being watched.

I look around, surreptitiously, not seeing anyone overtly looking my way. The feeling is impossible to shed.

I wonder if Gavin is somewhere in the room, watching, laughing as he torments his date, maybe discreetly recording the event to post online and shame Lara. The depths to which people will go to hurt someone are endless, and expanding technology multiplies the available means.

I find my anger outpacing my curiosity. I want to meet Gavin but am reluctant to go. If I leave, then I may never find my answers. And tomorrow, or the next day, I'll open my eyes inside another body further removed from my previous life.

Now people are looking at me. Not just the staff, who want to clear the table for the next guests, but other diners as well. A few women give me a compassionate look that obviously says, *I've been there*. A few guys glance in my direction before quickly looking away. I'm not sure if they're feeling guilty because they're on a date and checking me out, or if they're thinking about dates they've stood up in the past.

Or maybe nobody's thinking anything, and I'm getting worked up over nothing. I'm usually good at reading people, at taking a room's pulse, but tonight I'm off my game — anxious over feeling so close yet so far from a clue.

I finish my water, push back my chair, leave a twenty dollar bill on the table for taking up space, then leave.

On the drive back to my apartment, I glare out the window, wondering what happened to my date.

Had he come and left? Maybe something held him up and kept him from meeting me. I begin arguing with myself.

He could've called.

Yeah, but maybe his phone was dead.

Still, he could've used someone else's phone, right? Or does he work alone in an underground silo?

I search Lara's available memories and realize that she has no idea what this guy does for a living.

Who agrees to meet a guy when she clearly knows so little about him? Have some standards, girl.

I swing by a drive-through burger joint on the way home, then make my way to Lara's. I open the door, eager to eat my burger and leave the night behind me.

I turn on the lights, then close and lock the door. I set my sack of food on the kitchen counter and look at the answering machine to see if maybe Gavin left a message.

A red number one flashes.

I head to the machine when I suddenly realize I'm not alone.

I turn around and see a man standing right behind me.

I jump back, startled, putting distance between us.

The man stands there staring at me.

One of the problems that comes with jumping is that I'm often surprised by people in my host's home. Sometimes, it'll be a relative; other times a good friend or a lover. It always takes a moment to realize who the person is in relation to my host. I have to drown the temporary shock of seeing a stranger, chalking it up to being temporarily startled, and do my best not to overreact until my host fills me in on the person's details.

I smile awkwardly waiting for Lara to fill me in and let me know who this person is.

He is in his early thirties, tall, lanky, wearing baggy black pants and a black tee beneath a larger red shirt. He has his hands in his pants pockets, completely casual. His face is gaunt, dark circles under his eyes, scraggly curly brown hair hanging in his eyes. He's looking at me with the oddest expression, like a child fascinated by seeing a deer frolic into his yard.

I'm waiting for Lara to fill me in.

But nothing comes.

Who the hell is this guy, and how did he get in here?

"Hello?" I ask, trying not to sound too confused in case I should know him.

"Hello, Lara." The voice is instantly recognizable — Gavin.

I step back. Fear and confusion bubble through my system. This isn't the guy in the photo on my phone. But there's something else, too — that sensation that I *know* this man. Not Lara, but I — or one of the people I have been — knows him.

"Gavin? How did you get in here?"

He smiles, then pulls gloved hands from his pockets.

Oh, God.

He's on me before my body can react, hands around

my throat, choking me, shoving me back against the refrigerator.

I try to scream, but nothing much comes out.

I kick, scratch, and claw, but his grip only grows stronger, tightening like a vise. His brown eyes bore into mine. And inside them, I see something … *familiar.*

And then it hits me — I've seen these eyes before. In this exact same context.

Gavin has attacked one of my hosts before. I can't remember which one, but I feel it with an unshakeable certainty. And if I don't stop him, he's going to kill Lara.

That realization sparks a fiery adrenaline through my body. Thrashing, my heel manages to kick him hard in his kneecap.

He screams, releasing my throat as he clutches at the pain.

I fall to the ground and scramble desperately toward my bedroom. I can't make it to the front door because he's standing between me and it. The bedroom is a terrible option, but also my only one.

Somehow I make it.

I turn to close and lock the door. I'm not sure how many seconds it will buy me or how I'll escape, but it doesn't matter.

He's there.

Holding a knife.

Before I can react, the blade is inside me, plunging into my gut.

Pain and confusion battle as I feel something I've never felt before — my host returning to her body.

She's crying out, "Why?" over and over as we stumble back and fall onto the bed.

My control over Lara is gone.

I can't tell if she is asking *me* why or Gavin. I can't tell how much she's aware of, or whether she even senses me inside her.

I feel a wave of guilt imagining how this must feel, suddenly waking to this stranger stabbing her. Does she know this is Gavin?

She's looking up at him, gasping for air.

The taste of copper floods her throat, spilling out of her lips as she chokes. I can feel it, along with her fear, pain, and confusion, but the sensations seem muted. It's as if Lara being back in her body has dampened my ability to feel, like a splitter cable weakening a signal's overall strength.

I try willing her to get up. To fight back. To do something!

I'm powerless.

All she can do is stare up at Gavin.

Come on, Lara! Get up. We're not dead yet!

The monster glares down, watching the life bleed from her body.

Suddenly, movement behind him, at the bedroom door.

Allie!

Allie races toward him with a knife in her hand, screaming.

We're saved!

He dodges out of the way.

Allie stumbles toward us, falling to the bed beside us, knife tumbling from her fingers toward the pillows.

She looks up, eyes wide, realizing that she dropped the knife.

She reaches for it.

Then she's yanked hard, by her hair, off of the bed.

Gavin spins her around, punches her in the side of the head.

She collapses to the ground.

He kicks, though I can't see where — she's now out of view.

The viciousness on his face feels like another knife in my gut. I have to stop him. He'll kill us all!

I scream, but Lara's mouth offers no breath.

Lara's no longer in her body. She's dying.

While I vaguely remember having been this man's victim before, I can't recall what happened next. Did he kill my host? Or did she black out and I woke in someone else?

If I'm in a body when it dies, what happens to me?

I don't know and am terrified to find out.

Panic swells like raging fire. I'm helpless to do anything but watch from behind Lara's vacant eyes.

Gavin turns his attention back to us.

He sits beside us on the bed, staring into our eyes.

I feel violated in every sense of the word, unable to move, unable to stop whatever he's about to do.

He holds his stare, head tilted as if admiring his handiwork. Or maybe it's something else.

I feel like he's looking right past Lara and somehow into *my* eyes.

"You're not her," he says. "Who are you?"

I don't know if this is crazy talk or if he *can* actually see me.

I start to ask him what he means when he suddenly snaps.

"Stop staring at me!" he screams, as if he's talking directly to me — that he can see *me* in here, looking back at him.

He looks down at his blood-covered blade, then back at us, his face twisting from a calm facade to one of utter, uncontrollable rage.

"I said stop staring at me!"

He thrusts the knife forward, straight into our eyes.

The last thing I hear is him turning to Allie on the floor.

"Well, don't you look like a lot of fun," he says.

Chapter Two

SUNDAY

I'M GASPING for air as I wake, an urgency burning through my lungs.

A hand touches me in the dark. I scream, pushing myself away, falling off the bed, bumping my head into the wall.

A light flicks on, and a pudgy dark-haired man in his early forties rushes to me.

"Baby, are you okay?"

Tony.

My host's mind fills in the name. He looks scared as he tried to help me up.

Tony. Why does he look so familiar?

I realize it's Tony, Yvonne's boyfriend.

Which means I'm in Yvonne's body.

All at once, I remember everything that happened to me — to Lara — yesterday.

This is significant.

I've never woken in hosts who knew one another before. I've also never remembered so much of a prior day. I have two sets of experiences when occupying a body: the host's and my own. For instance, having dinner with my host's family is *the host's memories*. I'll often forget their memories as if I'm somehow returning them to their rightful owner before leaving the body. But then I have what I call *my personal memories*, things I'm doing on my own. This could be reading a book, seeing a TV show, or something that I initiate, and doesn't involve anyone else. These memories stay with me longer, which is good because I'm not sure how I'd exist with no sense of self. And it's how I can track my lost days — 357 so far.

Hosts' memories are usually washed away when I wake up, with the new host's memories supplanting the old ones. But today, Lara's memories are still my companion.

Tony is still looking at me nervously as he helps me stand.

I look at the clock.

7:12 a.m.

I remember the last thing I heard before Lara's life was snuffed out — the sound of Allie's scream.

I have to get to Lara's!

I hop out of bed, letting Yvonne's instincts drive me to the closet.

"What are you doing?" Tony asks.

"Gotta go to work."

"Work? You're off today."

"I forgot something I need to take care of," I tell him, surprised how fast the lie leaves my lips.

"Are you serious?"

I'm not sure why it's such a big deal, but judging from the hurt in Tony's voice it is. Is this something Yvonne does a lot, letting her work get in the way of their personal life? Or maybe today is a special day. Whatever the case, Yvonne's mind isn't filling in the gaps, and I don't have time for a conversation that might soothe Tony's injured ego. Whatever the fallout, I'll fix it later. Right now, I need to get dressed.

I throw on an oversized charcoal coat, grab Yvonne's phone and purse, then head out the door.

I find Yvonne's red Jeep, jump in, and squeal out of the parking garage.

For a moment, I'm not sure I'll remember where Lara lives, particularly in relation to Yvonne's apartment. Fortunately, her memories fill in the blanks, and I find myself at Lara's place in fifteen minutes.

Lara's apartment building, a ten-story structure in a quiet subdivision, looks like it probably would on any given Sunday morning. There are a few people walking their dogs, but for the most part the neighborhood is still in bed, or maybe making coffee.

I park, then race into the building.

Lara lives on the seventh floor. I debate which would be faster, taking the stairs or waiting for the elevator.

The elevator door dings open. A woman and four kids pour out in a clamor. Elevator it is.

As the elevator ascends, my heart is racing.

It occurs to me that I flew here without any plan. What will I do if the killer is still in Lara's apartment? Am I prepared to deal with Gavin? I have no idea what fighting skills my host has. Yvonne is short, slightly out of shape, and despite her bold personality, she doesn't strike me as a fierce fighter. By going to Lara's apartment am I adding another body to his list of victims?

Yvonne surprises me with a blast of memory.

An ex-boyfriend named Hector. Four years ago, his

possessiveness finally crossed the line. Despite a restraining order, he kept coming around. Once, after a particularly nasty exchange pushed her through a plate glass window. Yvonne wound up spending a month recovering in the hospital. After that, she realized that getting a gun was the only way to ensure her safety. That and going to the shooting range nearly every week and learning to use it.

I reach into her purse, hand closing around the pistol.

I thank Yvonne for being a badass. The elevator door dings open.

I head to Lara's apartment, gun in hand, safety off. Ready.

I approach the closed door, not sure exactly what to do next. Do I knock? Do I kick down the door? I reach out, turn the knob.

It twists open.

My heart is racing as I step over the threshold into the apartment, gun drawn.

The gun in hand feels natural thanks to Yvonne's muscle memory, but I'm not nearly as experienced. I vaguely recall using guns as other people, but don't think I've ever shot anyone. The thought of doing so, even to stop a killer, is turning my stomach.

My hand shakes as my mind circles a pair of concerns: either I'll see movement and pull the trigger on someone I shouldn't, or my hesitation to shoot the first thing I see will cost me if Gavin *is* in here, waiting with a gun of his own.

I push the fears from my mind and focus on the room.

The kitchen is to the right. As I look at the fridge, I get a flash of Gavin shoving me — Lara — against it.

The living room ahead looks more or less as it did before yesterday's invasion. The bedroom door is on the far side of the living room, closed.

There is where Lara's body likely waits.

But will I find another? Did the monster murder Allie, too?

I move toward the door. A convergence of feelings hits me — what Allie meant to both Lara and Yvonne, and how they thought of her as a friend, almost like a little sister. It only adds to my waiting dread.

Gun in hand, I reach out, turn the doorknob, and push the door open.

My breath catches as I see Lara's body sprawled on the bed, nude, eyes gouged out, peppered wounds up and down her body as if Gavin had stabbed her hundreds of times in his violent rage.

But Allie isn't here.

The smell of fluids is overwhelming: the metallic scent of blood, shit from opened bowels, and the dominant stench of piss reeking above it all.

I turn away, fighting the rising vomit in my throat.

Too late.

It comes out, adding to the room's horrible stench.

I stagger toward the bathroom to see if Allie's inside.

No sign of her here, either.

I set the gun on the counter, then spit into the sink. I turn on the faucet and lean forward to rinse my mouth out. As I stand back up, I catch a glimpse of a stranger in the mirror.

I grab the gun and spin around, but I'm alone.

Only then do I realize the stranger is Yvonne's reflection.

Despite her corpse on the bed, I'm still thinking of myself as Lara, which isn't how this usually works. Old identities rarely linger into a new host.

I can't get bogged down in what this means, though. I have to find out what happened to Allie. I grab the gun and inspect the apartment, finding neither her nor any sign of what might have happened. If he killed her too, I think he would've left her. But if Allie escaped, she would've called the sheriff's office by now. With no deputies or caution tape here, I doubt she got away.

My only other option is ugly, and I can't consider it yet.

I race out of the apartment and down the hall to Allie's, tucking the gun into my coat pocket.

I knock on the door, louder and more urgently than I intend to.

No answer.

Maybe her mom found Allie in the hallway, picked her up, drove her to the hospital? It's at least one possibility with a glimmer of hope.

I knock again.

A surly-sounding woman says, "Hold yer horses!"

The sound of locks sliding.

The door opens, though a security chain holds it from opening all the way.

Allie's mother, a bleached blonde with dark roots, bedhead, and a body worn ragged from years of drinking, answers. "Yeah?"

"Is Allie home?"

"Who's asking?" She eyeballs me through the crack in the doorway.

I don't have time to think of an answer that she won't find suspicious. So I blurt the truth.

"Your daughter may be in danger. Is she home?"

Her mother's eyes widen, and her surliness is replaced by a less guarded emotion — fear.

"Hold on," she says, closing the door, likely going to check.

It saddens but doesn't altogether surprise me, that her mother doesn't even know if her teenage daughter is home.

I hear the chain slide off. The door opens all the way.

"No, she's not home. What's this about?"

"There's no note or anything?"

"My daughter doesn't leave notes. What's going on?"

And now I have to face the ugly possibility head-on.

"I think someone may have taken your daughter."

AN HOUR LATER, I feel like I'm stuck in a nightmare of fading time as a detective questions me in a small interrogation room at the sheriff's office.

Of course, I can't tell him the truth.

Yes, I was in Lara's body when he murdered her.

Yes, I'm a Jumper. I'm in a different person every day or so.

What? You'd like to escort me to the psychiatric wing for an evaluation? Whatever for?

I have to invent a lie that will hold up — and give them enough details to maybe find this bastard.

I offer every bit of information I can, down to Gavin's name and description, to the best of my memory. Details feel fuzzy when I try to recall his specific features. Was his nose wide or thin? Was his chin pointed or round? How long was his hair? I was so focused on his eyes — black, familiar, and cold — that the rest of him is a blur. But I give my best approximation to the sketch artist capturing details.

When asked how I know what he looked like, or how I know he was the one who did this to Lara, I have to lie, saying I went to her apartment after hearing nothing about her date. I said that she'd normally call me to let me know if things were going well, or horribly.

When I didn't hear from her, I stopped in. She answered the door, and they were in the kitchen talking.

Lara seemed uncomfortable, but nothing that seemed — at the time — too alarming. I figured she was nervous finally meeting a guy she'd been talking to for so long.

I *could have* just said that I saw his picture on Lara's phone, and I know that women will look out for each other when they go on blind dates so maybe the lies aren't necessary, but instinct is all that I have and I follow it like a trail of breadcrumbs, spinning this web of lies, knowing I'm screwing Yvonne once she returns to her body.

From what little I know of police investigations, and subsequent trials, this is only Yvonne's first round of questions. What happens when I'm not here and our answers don't match? Will that turn her into a suspect? Will it make the case against Gavin, assuming they can catch him, fall apart?

As a Jumper, the number of variables beyond my control can feel paralyzing. I'll often choose to do nothing for fear of whatever chain of events in my host's life I might inadvertently set into motion. But this time *nothing* isn't an option.

The deputies need to find Allie, assuming Gavin hasn't killed her.

When Detective Ramirez asks how I knew Allie was even at the house, I tell him that she was there earlier, and would likely be spending the night since her mother was a drunk.

"You're saying this girl would spend the night even though Lara had brought a date home?" Ramirez asks. "That doesn't seem a bit odd to you?"

"Lara was a kind person. She wouldn't turn Allie away just because she had a date. If anything, she'd probably include her. Maybe the three of them would watch a movie or something, then Lara would send Gavin home with a peck on the cheek."

I don't know if my story is holding water. It's tough to get a bead on Ramirez. He's in his early fifties, has a buzz-cut which suggests military service, and looks like he's spent a lifetime interviewing liars.

I can't help but feel like he sees right through me.

As the paper's editor, Yvonne has history with Ramirez and several other officers. Some respect and like her; others dislike Yvonne for her editorials which are often critical of the current sheriff's administration. Ramirez has always been a straight shooter, never getting involved in politics. He respects Yvonne. Which is good, as it's probably the only thing keeping him from seeing through my lies.

After a while, the sketch artist shows me her drawing of the suspect. I *think* it looks like him, I say. Judging from her frown, she's not happy with my uncertainty. I'm afraid they might not use the sketch, so I insist that it looks like him. I say I'm almost positive, even though I'm more like 40 percent certain.

His eyes are deadly accurate.

The sketch artist leaves. Detective Ramirez thanks me, and says he'll be in touch. He gets up to escort me out of the interview room.

"Wait," I say, "what are the odds of finding Allie alive?"

"I dunno," he says, shaking his head. "Our deputies are out now doing their best."

"Is there anything I can do?"

"Call me if you think of anything else that might help. Also, get with Celine. She'll give you a press release you can put on your website."

Celine is Sheriff Ben Dixon's spokeswoman, a glorified flack who hates Yvonne because she never swallows the sheriff's official bullshit. Yvonne presses her for information, unlike the daily paper, which spends half its editorial ink licking local politico ass. Memories are filling in the blanks: just how much Yvonne distrusts the sheriff department's ability to close this case — to find Allie alive.

I sigh. Tears sting my eyes. If I leave now, no one will ever find Gavin. "There has to be something else."

"Listen, I know this is hard on you. You lost Lara, and Allie might be in danger, too. I get it. But we've got our best people on it."

Snippets of memories flood into the front of my brain.

This isn't the first unsolved murder this year. There have been two others, both women. Both of them mutilated. The sheriff's office had been downplaying a serial killer, which is one of the things the paper had been pressing Dixon on for some time.

I look at Ramirez. "Do you think this is related to the other unsolved murders?"

"Don't go there."

"Why?" I ask, standing between him and the exit. Now he's the one being questioned.

"Listen, Yvonne. I'm not saying anything on record. You want quotes, go to Celine."

"Come on, Hector," I say, using his first name to sway him.

He smiles, shakes his head, and presses past me to the doorway. "We're doing our best. That's all you're getting outta me."

I storm out of the room, pissed, but I keep my anger inside. Ramirez is doing his job. He's one of the good guys, and I'm sure whatever part of the case he's involved in, he'll do his best to get Allie back. Still, I wish there was something I could do.

I had the bastard, Gavin, right there in front of me. I could've stopped him before he killed Lara. Before he did

God only knows what to Allie. I *should* have stopped him. Now Lara is dead, and Allie's about to join her, or already there.

I remember his glare, the hate in his gaze as he plunged the knife into Lara's eyes. So much hate, and for what? What would lead a person to commit such violence upon another?

I've been in a few hundred people now, many of them going through terrible shit, abuse from a loved one, drug addiction, depression. It's never easy to deal with. I know there are theories on the cycle of abuse, parents turning their children into monsters who grow up to be killers and rapists. I can understand on some level that we can't hold these monsters to the same standards as everyone else, but hell if I can understand what pushes anyone into murdering an innocent. You'd think they have some compassion as a victim themselves. Why not go after the people who harmed you, or go after other horrible people? Why target someone who never hurt you?

I sit in the Jeep outside the sheriff's office, not ready to leave just yet. I look at the time on my phone: *10:40 am*. It's still relatively early, but I can't help feeling like time is ticking too fast. The longer Allie is missing, the less likely it is she'll be home.

There must be *something* I can do.

I thumb through the contacts in Yvonne's phone, hoping that one of them will trigger a memory of my temporary time as someone who can help. As I scan names, many of them her sources, Yvonne's memories fill in the gaps. This guy is a Civil War expert. This woman is a specialist in medicine. This one is an environmental activist. Her contacts list is long, populated with people who could help her on nearly any story she and her reporters might need to tackle, but none seem to have a skill set that can help us find Allie.

Ramirez had assured me that his people would be following every lead. At the moment, their best bet seems to be Lara's phone records. If they could trace the guy's number to a legitimate phone, rather than some prepaid burner, they might get a name and address. The detectives were also reaching out to the site where Lara met Gavin. If they could get an IP address, they could trace it back to him. But again, this was assuming he didn't go through proxies or find another method of hiding his location. Even after talking online for months, he's surely obscured his trail.

So much going on and so little I can help with.

I decide to leave, though I have no idea where I'm going. I'm off today, and while Yvonne will have to get with her bosses to find a replacement for Lara, that isn't my problem. I don't want to go home. Tony might still be there, and I don't feel like interacting with anyone, particularly while having to maintain appearances that I am who I'm pretending to be.

I need to be alone, to clear my head, to analyze what's happened and see if I can't figure something out.

I drive to a park with a winding four-mile jogging path and get out of the Jeep. Nothing like a brisk walk to get my thoughts flowing.

It's still cool enough outside that I can wear my jacket without drawing too much attention. It's not like I think Gavin will show up at the park and suddenly come after me, but at the moment, I'd prefer the peace of mind that comes with my concealed firearm.

I pick up the path along the edge of the parking lot and follow it along the outskirts of a baseball diamond. The park isn't too crowded this morning, mostly moms pushing their infants and toddlers in strollers, some older people on the tennis courts, and a few random walkers and joggers. For the most part, I avoid prolonged eye contact or the exchanging of pleasantries with strangers.

As I walk a bit farther, the path splits in two directions. One continues around the park and eventually back to the parking lot. The other extends through a wooded area that makes up the park's northern half, turning into a nature trail.

I head into the woods.

There's something about walking in nature that always calms my mind. Being surrounded by the various trees, plants, insects, birds — an entire ecosystem that exists away from direct human influence — puts me in a relaxed state of mind that I can rarely find among people and their problems.

I'm playing these other parts so often. Being other people leaves me no room for myself. But among the trees, there's no need to pretend that I'm anyone other than the soul resting deep inside the body. It's the only time I can walk the world as myself.

I keep walking, listening to buzzing insects and chirping birds, branches bowing gently in the wind, letting it all envelop me. I wish I could stop time and live in this moment forever.

It's not luxurious, decadent, or any of the things people enjoy so much. And yet it's greater than all of those things — these quiet moments of being my real self in the world.

Eventually, my mind returns to last night's terror. While some of Lara's memories are fuzzy, they're sticking better than any previous host's. I'm not sure why I'm able to recall so much of yesterday — if it has something to do with the traumatic way in which Lara died, or if there's some part of her that carried over with me into Yvonne's body.

I'm not sure if I believe in a soul in the religious sense, as this separate part of us that goes on to Heaven or Hell when we die, but I know there *is* some part of us that exists beyond our flesh and blood. My existence and my current state of body jumping are proof. And since I have no better word for it, I'm calling it soul. And despite not having a physical body, and brain, the soul remembers. It's how I'm able to remember bits of other hosts' lives, even if I can't recall a splinter of my own. It's how, I think, I can still access Lara's memories — because part of her soul is still with me.

I've often wondered what happens to the host's soul when I'm occupying their body. Is it there, watching but unable to do anything to stop the uninvited puppeteer? Or does it go somewhere else? Maybe they enter my body, wherever it is, like some sort of body swap.

I guess that their soul returns when I leave. While I've never run into someone after I've been in their body, I have looked a few people up online to ensure that they're still alive and kicking, not locked away in some mental home. I've read journals and blog posts from people I've been in, searching for some clue as to whether they were aware of what had happened. I've yet to find any entries that said, "Oh, man, someone else took over my body yesterday" or "I woke up in someone else's body" or anything like that. My guess is that somehow their brains are accommodating whatever happened to them, threading my memories into theirs for a seamless transition. I have no proof and have yet to work up the courage to contact someone I've been in and ask them what happened.

I'm not sure why, but the thought of doing so overwhelms me with an urgent sense of dread. Like something or someone telling me, *don't do it, or you'll screw things up.*

And if there's one thing I've learned over the past year it's to trust my gut on all things. Our instincts are aware of so much more than our surface selves, and I'm sure there's something inside me that understands what's happening to me even if my brain hasn't yet figured it out.

Again, I find myself wondering if Lara's soul is still with me, now in Yvonne's body.

I try to access random memories from Lara's past, ones I hadn't accessed yesterday — ones I'd be seeing for the first time. This could prove that I'm somehow tapped into some part of Lara that still lives on. But everything I see in her memories is a jumbled, fuzzy mess, and I can't tell if a snippet from her childhood is something I came across yesterday, or am accessing now for the first time.

But given how much of Lara I feel inside me, I feel both her compulsion to save Allie and an obligation to avenge her murder and bring justice to Gavin.

I'm chilled, remembering the way Gavin looked not *at* Lara, but *through* her, as if he could see me inside of her. I don't know if this is in my head or not, but coupled with my recognition of his voice, and that he's killed one of my hosts before, I know there's something at play here.

A horrible thought washes over me.

What if it wasn't a host he'd killed before? What if it was *me* — the disembodied lost soul — floating from person to person? What if *my* body is dead and there's no way I can ever return? What if this vagabond life is my hellish eternity?

While this isn't the first time I've contemplated that I might be some a ghost, the theory has never felt right. I've always believed that there had to be some other explanation and that this is a temporary state — someday I'll have a normal life, back in my own body. I don't know why I cling to that hope. Maybe because the alternative is too depressing.

If this is my life, then what's the point of living?

I'm not living *my* life; I'm trapped in a borrowed existence. Waking up in homes that aren't mine, making memories that will never belong to me, falling in love with people who don't know who I am, and will be gone when I open my eyes the next morning. This isn't a life; this is an unending series of Could Have Beens, and in the end, if there ever is one, what do I, as a person, have to show for it?

Nothing but fuzzy memories of lives lived by proxy.

My mood darkens. Misery threatens to throw me over the edge.

I remind myself of the positives. There are many lives I've been in for a day or two that were thoroughly miserable. At least I'm not stuck living out their full existence. I bet these unfortunate souls would trade everything to swap lives every day or so. I get to see humanity from different sexes, races, and lifestyles, to experience every flavor of reality in a way that no other person ever has before.

Despite the *opportunity*, I still feel like shit.

As much as I try to polish this turd enough to see the bright side, it doesn't change my eternal loneliness. Every connection I make, every friendship I forge, is for naught. I'm doing all the work while others reap the rewards.

And now I'm not even helping others. I've cost Lara her life. Allie may be next if she's not already dead.

I need to do something. But what?

I can't go to the *Chronicle*. Not now. Too many people will need me to do too many things. And, frankly, I don't know what to do. Not yet.

I decide to head home since I know Tony will be at work.

Once there, I hit the Internet hard, searching for anything I can find in the news, stories about unsolved murders of women and kidnappings in the area, as well as along the West Coast — something I can maybe use to find a clue that might lead me to Gavin and Allie.

I find a few stories, but nothing that helps me, unless my goal is to know how vicious the world can be, and how many atrocities go unsolved each day.

To make matters worse, as I'm trying to read, bits of Lara's memories gathered yesterday keep running through my head. They're not even useful memories, just random events. Once she had a dog named Snuffles who ran away when she was seven. She likes when ice cream is partially melted, so it's almost like a milkshake. She and Allie once spent an entire Saturday watching *Mystery Science Theater 3000* while devouring three bags of Doritos and drinking soda, and that was maybe one of the most fun days she'd had as an adult. Those and tons of other little memories that only serve to distract me and make me feel horrible.

I shouldn't have agreed to meet Gavin. Had I just stayed home, like I wanted, Lara might be alive. Allie might be safe at home, or at least sheltered on Lara's couch.

But no, I allowed my needs to come before my host's — my need to find out why Gavin's voice was so familiar.

And what did my selfishness get me? No answers, a dead woman cut down in the prime of her life, and a missing child who may never escape her misery into happier days.

A wave of guilt has gone out to sea only to gather enough strength to return as a tsunami.

I violated my number one rule — not to mess with people's lives.

I am useless.

I am worse than useless.

I hurt these people. My actions will ripple, and be felt forever by those who knew them.

I head to the kitchen and am not disappointed to find Yvonne's wine rack filled with many worthy bottles of alcohol.

I drink at first to forget the pain.

Then I drink to fall asleep before I can do more damage to these people.

Chapter Three

❦

I WAKE up feeling like I've taken all the neighborhood's drugs and drunk all the alcohol a human can possibly consume and still live to talk about it.

My host spent the night like Keith Richards, but *I'm* paying the price this morning. Assuming it's morning.

I open my eyes to look for a clock. Instead, I see what has to be one of the world's most beautiful women lying in bed beside me. She's Russian, with long brown hair and large green eyes. She's wide awake and staring as if waiting for me to get up.

She smiles. Her hand reaches beneath the sheets to find my cock. "You're up," she says with a porn star's purr.

Suddenly, another hand, behind me, reaches down, and a second woman coos, "Yes, he is."

I turn to see a Latin girl with long black hair and beautiful brown eyes — my girlfriend, Rosa, who apparently doesn't mind if we bring other women to bed.

"I thought you were gonna sleep forever," Rosa says, looking like she's been awake just a bit longer than I have.

It takes me a moment, but finally, details spill forth.

My name is Vincent (Vinnie) Fortunato. I'm thirty-one, and apparently, this is an everyday thing. Officially, I work at The Emerald Club, an exclusive *gentleman's club* in Bay Cove, frequented by athletes, stars, and mobsters. Unofficially, I'm a soldier for Sal Bruno, a local mobster.

The Russian is one of Vinnie's favorite dancers, Katerina, though she's hardly the only one who has shared our bed.

I look around Vinnie's spacious bedroom; massive bed, a flowing water sculpture, an 85-inch LCD TV, and abstract paintings hanging on the wall. But no clock, not anywhere.

Then I see my cell on the nightstand to Rosa's right. "Can you get me my phone?"

She hands it to me. I press the power button and see the time. Four eighteen in the afternoon.

Shit, it's so late.

I immediately think of Allie and wonder if the deputies have made any headway on her case. I'm still in Clay County, though in the more populated southern part. The fact that I'm still in Bay Cove is an unprecedented third time in the same locale. I can't help but feel like this is intentional, that the force controlling me is *choosing* to keep me here. If that is the case, I have to ask, why? Is this force giving me some ability to find Allie?

First, I woke up as Yvonne, the one person who could describe Gavin to the sheriff's deputies without drawing suspicion, which had to be a huge help in finding Allie.

Nobody else could have pushed the case forward like that. Right?

So now I'm Vinnie Fortunato, a mobster.

How the hell can you help me find Allie?

How am I supposed to pull off being a mobster?

I've woken in the bodies of criminals before but have never been part of an organized crime family. Suddenly, I'm overwhelmed with thoughts of what this job might entail — extortion, assault, murder?

"You all right?" Rosa asks.

"Still recovering. My head is pounding, and my throat is tore up. Can you get me something?"

I'm careful not to specify a particular drug, as that's one of those details that could give me away, or at least trigger confusion.

Aspirin? You never take aspirin! In fact, you're allergic to aspirin. Who are you?

Rosa gets up and heads to the bathroom.

Katerina, meanwhile, reaches back down, trying to coax me into continuing last night's fun.

"No. Not now."

I'm short with her. Not rude, but not overly kind. I can feel that Vinnie keeps most people at a distance. I'm not sure if this is how he's hardwired, not to trust anyone too much, or a method to keep women interested. Probably both.

Katerina looks wounded, gets up, searches for her dress on the ground, and slinks out of the room.

Both girls are stunning, and any guy would be lucky to wake up between them, but I can't bring myself to capitalize on the offer. That's not to say I've never had sex with anyone while in a host. There have been a few times, but they've never been with someone the host was already in a relationship with. To me, it's a violation on many levels, to have sex with someone the host knows. I'd be taking advantage of an existing union, and tricking the person. Strangers, or someone the host is just meeting, are fair game. In those cases, I don't feel like I'm lying.

It's one of my codes, even if it's harder than most to live by. Sometimes, particularly when I'm in a body for a few days, it's hard to find excuses to turn someone down that won't cause problems in the relationship. I also come to feel for some of these people. It's only natural. And the more I like them, the harder it is not to crave physical connection.

Rosa returns, hands me three white pills, then pulls a bottle of cold water from a mini fridge in the nightstand.

"Here ya go."

She sits beside me on the bed while I look at the pills. They don't have a recognizable logo or name, and I'm guessing they're painkillers, probably the kind Vinnie would normally use for recreation.

I want to numb this headache, without feeling the euphoria that might dull my thoughts. I need to look for connections, to find some way that Vinnie, or someone he knows, might help me find Allie.

I take one pill and put the other two on the nightstand, hoping that doesn't draw too much attention.

Why are you only taking one? You usually take three just to get up at the crack of four. You're not Vinnie!

I swallow the pill then take a swig of the cold water, which feels like heaven to my dry, cracked throat. I'm surprised how thirsty I am and gulp down the bottle.

Rosa doesn't say anything about me taking one pill.

We sit there for a moment, uncomfortably silent. It makes me wonder what kind of relationship Vinnie and Rosa have. Is it a good sign that they can both sit there quietly, just enjoying one another's company? Or is he a controlling asshole who doesn't let his woman speak? I can't plug into his feelings for her.

She's staring down at the sheets at first, but then she looks up at me and smiles. Not an awkward smile, but one that suggests a solid relationship. That's good. Because one of my other codes is to act like my host, so as not to draw attention. If the host is an asshole, I can't go around being nice and giving people lavish gifts and shit to make up for the host's usual cruelty. It would be unkind in its own way, giving people a place to hang their hope, a reason to stay in a relationship they might otherwise leave.

Oh, look, he's not so bad. I can make this work.

If anything, I'd rather be meaner, maybe push someone out of a bad relationship, if I don't think it'll do more harm than good once the host returns. But I have no line on how a mobster handles a woman leaving him. Would he be compelled to put a hit on her or something? It's best to keep the status quo.

"What?" Rosa asks, knowing my wheels are turning.

"Nothin'. Just looking at you."

She leans forward and kisses me.

Kissing a lover or spouse is one of the trickiest parts of this gig. Kisses are personal. I feel guilty for violating the host's relationship. But I can't pull away without harm. And I never quite know how the host kisses. Involve the tongue, and it's like a dance where you have to follow your partner's lead. Go too soft or too aggressive, and suddenly the kiss becomes a disaster, and the other person is looking at you like the stranger you are.

That's not how you normally kiss! What's going on?

Fortunately, Rosa's kiss is a soft, yet tender, peck on the lips. Amazing how much I can tell from a kiss. In Rosa's, I can feel her genuine affection for Vinnie. I'm not yet sure what kind of guy Vinnie is, but whatever is going on between him and Rosa, it's good.

She looks at me. "I'll let you get ready for your meeting. I'll take Katerina home, okay?"

Thanks to my splitting headache, I can play up my *forgetfulness*. "What meeting?"

"With Gray. At six. You forget?"

A name pops into my head, Duncan Gray, a Bay Cove city councilman. Why he's meeting with Vinnie, though, I don't know.

"Yeah, totally spaced on it," I say, hoping I'm sounding close to how I feel like Vinnie talks.

Sometimes when I'm in people, I can hear their voice, memories, like best-of clips, running through their brains, replaying old conversations. This is helpful when it comes to sounding like my host. But sometimes people think in words they'd never use in public. One time I was in a straight-laced prim and proper fifty-year-old bank manager named Susan. Her head was filled with gangsta rap lyrics. She thought of her customers as bitches that needed to get stitches. I assume she normally kept those thoughts to herself. I wasn't going to put her job at risk by attempting to talk like that. Though, I did find myself laughing at her mostly inappropriate thoughts throughout the day. Those eight hours were a struggle. It's a miracle I managed to keep her job.

Rosa leaves the bedroom, and I finally get out of bed.

As I shower and dress, I cull Vinnie's memories for details of my meeting with the councilman. Apparently, there's a big exchange about to take place. I'm supposed to hand over a flash drive with incriminating photos and videos of a local church pastor, James Wilson, engaged in some less than Godly behavior.

How Vinnie got the evidence, or why Councilman

Gray wants it, I don't know. I'm probably working under the auspices of Mr. Bruno.

After my shower, I dry off and head into a huge walk-in closet, greeted with perhaps the most expensive clothing I've ever seen in a man's wardrobe. I choose a pair of fitted charcoal trousers and a white dress shirt. I vaguely recognize some of the brands, while others I've never heard of. Everything is exquisitely tailored. Probably bespoke.

I dress in the full-length mirror and admire Vinnie's physique. He parties hard but has the kind of body that requires daily hours in the gym to maintain. He's broad-shouldered, with olive skin and a killer smile. He could be a movie star — if he wasn't a mobster.

Part of me feels bad for whatever circumstances have led Vinnie down such a narrow road. I can feel his discomfort, how he feels trapped by his life.

Sometimes, life feels like a lottery.

It's not just the sum and substance of the person that determines the station they'll rise to. It's the connections they make or fail to make, that seal their fate.

If things had been different, Vinnie could be an entrepreneur, a movie star, or some other legitimate success. He has the charm, looks, and drive to get what he wants.

But he could also be working a soul-crushing blue-collar job, struggling to put food on his family's table.

There are endless variables between What Is and What Could Have Been.

Being in so many people's shoes, I've seen the same thing countless times: people with obvious talent, the right looks, or some other quality that gives them a genetic advantage over others, yet they fail to capitalize on what they have. Sometimes, it's because they were programmed to fail early in their life by shitty parents or hateful, jealous peers. Other times, they never found a reason to believe in themselves, to reach outside their corner of the world, and look for more.

From the bits I can grasp of his troubled youth, I'm thinking that for Vinnie, this *is* him making the most of his opportunities.

This is the best he could've done.

I shudder as bits of his memories flitter by. I can tell that he's used to shoving them down. It's how he gets through his days, how he does what he has to do: ignore how it makes him feel and push through.

After I get dressed, I head to Vinnie's home office, find the flash drive on his desk, and am about to put it in his laptop, curious to see what kind of dirt they have on the holy man.

On second thought, I don't want to know what's on the flash drive. It can't be good. And I can't screw with whatever plans Mr. Bruno and Gray are concocting without putting Vinnie in danger with his boss.

I slip the drive into my pocket and instead search the web for anything new on Allie's disappearance.

There's nothing.

I go to the *Chronicle's* website to see if they have anything new.

There is an obituary for Lara, which I can't bring myself to read. I'm already feeling like hell for what happened to her. I don't need to feel worse.

I *need* to find Allie.

How can you help me find her, Vinnie?

Getting nothing, and growing frustrated sitting at his laptop staring at Lara's photo, I decide to head out for my meeting with Councilman Gray. But first I slip on Vinnie's shoulder holster and a jacket to conceal his gun.

~

WE MEET at the Bay Cove Resort and Marina, in an underground parking lot.

I pull Vinnie's red Corvette up beside the councilman's black BMW and get out.

I climb into his car.

Duncan Gray is in his fifties, and looks like a cross between a trusted family doctor and a TV actor, with a kindly face and good looks that only become more distinguished as he ages.

"Hello, Mr. Fortunato," he says, shaking my hand and smiling.

I can't figure out how well these two know one another, but I get a feeling that Vinnie is often the conduit between the councilman and Mr. Bruno. I'm not sure if this is to protect Mr. Gray's reputation from associating with a known mobster or to protect Mr. Bruno's from associating with a politician. Maybe Mr. Bruno is more of a behind-the-scenes mob boss.

"Mr. Gray," I say with a firm shake.

"As promised."

He hands me a thick manila envelope. I assume it's stuffed with cash, but I don't open it. I slip it into my jacket pocket then retrieve the flash drive and hand it over.

Councilman Gray takes it, his eyes transfixed as if I handed him the Holy Grail.

"Tell Mr. Bruno thank you. This is going to make a lot of people very happy."

I nod, not entirely sure what he's talking about, but pretending that I do. I resist the urge to ask what's on the drive. It's either assumed that I know or it's above my pay grade. Either way, knowing won't help me find Allie.

I say, "I'll be sure to relay that," then get out of the councilman's car feeling like I need to shower.

~

I DRIVE AROUND AIMLESSLY after leaving the councilman, trying to make connections with nothing.

Without meaning to, I find myself in the *Chronicle* parking lot, sitting in the car, wanting to go in. The office lights are on, but I can't tell for sure who's working. I see Yvonne's Jeep in the parking lot, along with a few other cars I don't recognize.

I'm not sure why, but I feel like if I can talk to Yvonne, maybe we can put our heads together and figure something out. She seems like a resourceful person, and if someone outside of the sheriff's department is going to find Allie, my money's on her.

But I can't just walk into the offices and offer my help. For one, I doubt Yvonne's alone, and I can't talk to her with others around. And that's assuming she's receptive to what I'd have to say. For all I know, her yesterday is a blur. Maybe she's even wondering why she lied to the detectives and is today recanting those lies.

Yeah, but maybe that's why I should go in and talk to her. Help her put things together.

I push the button and turn off the car.

Am I really going to do this?

I open the door.

Then my phone rings.

I find it in my pocket, next to the envelope, and look at the name on the screen: *J. Jones.*

The bossman's alias.

I answer, heart racing.

"How did it go?" Mr. Bruno sounds older than I

expect, his Italian accent much thicker than Vinnie's almost nonexistent one.

"I gave him the … *package*. He said thank you; it will make a lot of people very happy."

Mr. Bruno laughs. "Yeah, I bet it will."

I'm not sure what that means, and I'm not about to ask.

"And I trust that he gave you something?"

"Yes, sir. I've got it with me."

"Okay, just bring it to the club tonight. Put it in the safe."

"Yes, sir."

And just like that, the line goes dead. No goodbye.

I sit there, waiting, in case he calls back. But no, this is how Mr. Bruno is. Short and to the point. No need for niceties.

There's movement in the office.

The front door opens. Yvonne steps out with two reporters. She locks the door. They pile into her Jeep, probably headed to dinner. Another late night.

No way I'll get her alone now.

I drive to the club feeling utterly useless.

AT THE CLUB, I head to the manager's office for some much-needed alone time. I need time to decompress and dissect everything that's happened today. I also don't know the first thing about running a strip club, or how Vinnie usually conducts business. It's best to hide for a while.

The office is a small, relatively quiet (you can still hear the dull thumping bass), bunker-like room in the club's basement, beneath the dancers' dressing rooms, practically the perfect place to sequester myself. There's a desk with a computer station seated in front of a wall of monitors showing the feeds from twenty-four security cameras around and outside the club. The view is a voyeur's wet dream — screens of women in various stages of undress, misbehaving drunks, and strippers grinding on men and women both in the champagne room. There are another four screens, turned off.

I reach out and turn one of them on.

It shows a bedroom, somewhere in the club, with a man tied to a bed as a dominatrix whips him.

One of four Special VIP rooms.

I wonder how often Vinnie sits in this room watching debauchery. My guess is that he's so numb to everything he sees, and experiences, the monitors are as boring to him as factory feeds to a security guard.

I turn off the picture, figuring there must be a reason he keeps it dead — maybe in case someone else shows up in this room — and head to the large black safe anchored to the ground. I kneel to deposit the envelope, per Mr. Bruno's instructions.

I don't know the combination, so I reach out for the safe's dial, and touch it, hoping to trigger Vinnie's memories to guide me.

Numbers appear in my head.

I turn the dial, following Vinnie's muscle memory.

The safe clicks open.

I'm not sure what I expected to see inside. Definitely bags of cash, of which there are five. But I didn't anticipate the other stuff — hard drives, flash drives, and several sealed document envelopes.

I look back at the monitors then spot several servers under the desk. Then I realize what's going on. Vinnie is recording everything that happens in the club, saving captured indiscretions, and using them for blackmail.

I wonder if the pastor was a guest at The Emerald. I can't imagine someone with such a public profile, particularly one wrapped in morality, would ever come to the club. Athletes, celebrities, sure. But a *pastor*?

I start to wish I'd watched what was on the flash drive.

I slip Councilman Gray's envelope into the safe, close the door, and lock it.

I return to the desk and have a seat, staring at the wall of sin.

I find my attention turning to the four dead monitors. I wonder what's happening in those rooms, which high roller is paying to engage in their filthiest fantasies.

I'm tempted to turn on the monitors for a look, but something catches my attention — a white van parked behind the club. The alley is meant for deliveries only and has nowhere to park. I can't imagine anyone is making deliveries at eight o' clock. The lights are off, but I see someone sitting inside the van.

I reach for my phone, call Ty, the club's head of security.

"Hey, boss," he says, loud music thumping in the background.

"Hey, we expecting any deliveries now?"

"No, why?"

"I need you to check the back alley. White van, someone just sitting there."

"Okay," he says. "Wanna stay on the phone?"

"Yes," I say, anxiously.

Being in body after body, I have a feel for the rhythms of life, fate, or whatever you want to call it.

I find Ty on the security cameras — a large bald black man in a coal-colored suit who looks like a defensive lineman — and watch as he heads toward the club's rear exit.

My eyes follow him from one camera to another, past the champagne room, past the dressing rooms, through a door and down a hall where the VIP rooms are located, then to the back door.

"Boss, the door is open."

I see a shadow behind Ty. Three shadows.

I call out, but I'm too late.

Three men wearing all black and ski masks, corner him.

One of the men shoots Ty.

I scream.

One of the men picks up Ty's phone. He has an American accent, gruff voice. "Hello, Vinnie. How do you wanna do this? You wanna open the door and let us in, or do we have to shoot everyone in the place?"

"What do you want?"

"What the hell do you *think* we want?"

I don't know. Do they know what's in the safe?

"Money?"

"Bingo! Now, what's it gonna be?"

"I'll let you in. Nobody needs to die," I say, hoping Ty is just injured.

"Good choice. Now to be sure you're not calling the cops, I'm gonna stay on the phone with you. And don't even think about tripping a silent alarm. I see cops, and you're gonna be the first to get a bullet in the head. Understand?"

"Yes," I say.

Within seconds, there's a rap at the door.

On the phone, "Little pig, little pig, let me in."

I go to the door and unlock it.

The man on the phone steps in first, pistol in my face, and grabs my phone. He stuffs it into his jacket pocket.

One of the others searches me. He takes my pistol while the other shuts and locks the door.

I wonder if anyone heard the gunshot. I might have only heard it because I was on the phone. One of the men, not sure if it's the one who shot Ty, has a suppressor on his pistol. A suppressor doesn't completely silence a gun, of course. Someone might have heard it and may be calling the cops. The other security guards could be making their way to the office.

"Okay," the leader says. "Open the safe."

I wonder if these men are aware of what else is in the safe. Even if they're not, they sure as hell might be interested once they open it up. Anything valuable enough to be locked away is precious enough to steal.

I can't let that happen.

I stare into the leader's blue eyes.

"You know who you're ripping off?"

"Why do you think we're here?"

"So you also know that Mr. Bruno will never let you get away with this."

"Mr. Bruno ain't ever gonna know who did it. Now open that fucking safe."

"Your funeral." I chuckle, kneeling to spin the dial.

My heart is pounding.

My fingers fumble on the dial. I screw up and have to start over.

"Stop stalling," the leader barks.

I don't respond. I don't look at him. I start the sequence again.

The door clicks open.

"Out of the way," the leader says.

I stand up, stomach anxious at what they'll do when they see the safe's additional contents, including the envelope that Councilman Gray gave me.

One of the other two men drops in front of the safe with a black duffel bag and lets out a loud whoop.

"What have we got here?" He grabs two of the hard drives and shows his partners.

"Just backups of our data."

The man looks back in the safe. "That's a lot of backup. I call bullshit."

"Put 'em in the bag," the leader says.

"I wouldn't do that," I warn.

"Fuck you." The leader aims his pistol at me, looking for an excuse to shoot.

The man at the safe looks back, awaiting instruction from his boss.

"Put it all in the bag."

As the man loads up the sack, my stomach is in knots imagining these punks having access to everything on the hard drives. I have to find a way to get them back, but they've taken my gun, and there are three of them.

I feel Vinnie's body itching for use. In addition to the hours he puts in at the gym, he trains in two different martial arts.

As my mind flashes on his training, I see something else — perhaps an opportunity. A blade hidden in my belt buckle.

How did I miss this while getting dressed?

Normally, I wouldn't risk my host's life like this. I'd let the men take the money and the rest of what's in the safe, then hope they allowed me to live. But knowing what I know of Vinnie's life, I have a feeling that Mr. Bruno could hurt, or kill him, for letting these men rob the safe. Vinnie was supposed to fall on his sword like any good soldier.

Instead, I opened the safe.

I put Vinnie in this situation, so I need to get him out.

The man fills the sack then stands and starts toward the

other two men. He has the bag in his left hand, gun in his right.

My heart is racing. I can feel energy coursing through me, like a spring pushed to its limit, ready to release.

I pull the bladed belt buckle out with my left hand, step behind the man with the bag, and bring the blade to his neck in one quick swoop.

Vinnie's instincts guide my moves, almost kicking me from the driver's seat. If left to me, I'd be frozen in fear. But some part of Vinnie remains and is ready to act.

I reach down, grab the thief's right hand, raise the gun, slide my finger over his trigger finger, and fire at the leader.

Two shots to his chest.

He falls back.

The other man raises his gun, fires.

I keep the robber's body between us, taking shots as the man empties his pistol.

Once I hear the gun run out of ammo, my left hand slices the thief's neck.

I spring toward the gunman.

He throws his gun at me.

I swat it aside, then shove him backward against the wall, raising the blade to his throat.

I meet his scared dark eyes.

A question comes to me, as instinctual as my movements. "Who hired you?"

I press the blade against his neck to prove I'm not fucking around.

I hear coughing behind me. The leader is down, but not out.

I grab the man I'm interrogating, and spin him to use him as my shield as the leader fires his pistol.

His shots are off, not hitting me or my man-shield.

I rush forward, shoving the man in front of me.

He falls on the leader and traps the gun under his body.

I race forward, drop to my knees, slicing upward with my left hand straight into the leader's neck.

His eyes bulge as he gargles on his blood.

The final thief, on top of him, makes a grab for the gun.

I elbow him hard in the head.

He stumbles back, somehow managing to get the gun, raising it up and firing.

Fear, adrenaline, and anger swell inside. I'm enraged that these men would attempt to rob me and Mr. Bruno.

Don't they know who we are?

I know these feelings are Vinnie's, and I can't quite figure out how they're swirling through my head. Things don't usually happen this way. I'll occasionally tap into someone's personal bank, including their muscle memory, allowing me to do things I couldn't normally do, but this rarely comes with the host's residual emotions. And yet, somehow, a part of Vinnie is with me.

Just like Lara was.

The last of the thieves stares up at me, shaking, raising his hands, "Please, please, don't kill me. I'll tell you anything you want to know."

"Who hired you?"

"Some Russian guy. I don't know his name, I swear."

I drop down beside him, return the blade to his neck.

"I want a name."

"I swear, I don't know! Some fucking Russian. Told us to hit you. Told us you'd have at least a half million, and we'd split it."

"Did he mention the other stuff in the safe?"

The man looked at me, confused.

"The hard drives and flash drives. Did he tell you to get those?"

"No, he just told us to get everything in the safe. Didn't tell us what all would be in there. Please, please, don't kill me."

Before I can weigh in, Vinnie's hand drives the blade across the thief's throat.

I jump back as if trying to distance myself from the body who just murdered a man who had more or less surrendered, a man who died begging for his life.

I didn't mean to kill him.

I *didn't* kill him.

Did I?

I stumble back, dropping the blade, staring at the trio of bodies around me.

I see blood on the ground, then the blood staining my shirt.

One of the leader's shots *did* hit me. My abdomen's gushing.

And then, like the Coyote in those Road Runner cartoons running off a cliff and not falling until he realizes it, I *feel* the pain.

It's not nearly as bad as it probably should be. I'm not sure if this is a good thing, my adrenaline preventing me from feeling it, or a bad thing — a sign that I'm grievously injured.

I start toward the leader to retrieve my phone.

My legs are wobbly, my head dizzy. Terrible signs.

Please don't let another person die on my watch.

I fish the phone from his pocket, watching him the entire time as if he might spring to life like some horror movie monster.

He doesn't.

I sit on the ground, dial 9-1-1 and tell them to hurry — there have been several shootings.

As the operator asks me about my status, I look over to the bag the thieves had tried to steal and try crawling toward it, to put the bag in the safe and lock it before the sheriff's deputies show. I can hear Mr. Bruno yelling at Vinnie, "Clean up your fucking mess!"

My mind flashes on several *messes* Vinnie has had to clean in the past — how many bodies he's had to put down, had to bury for his boss.

The bag might as well be miles away. I can't move. Vinnie's body won't respond to a single signal that my brain is trying to send.

Come on, dammit!

The emergency operator tells me to hold on.

I remember the man in the van.

He's still there, waiting. What if he comes in for the bag?

I try willing myself toward the bag.

Instead, I fall face down to the ground.

Chapter Four

~

I WAKE UP IN DARKNESS, lying in a bed, dizzy.

At first, I think I'm still in Vinnie's body, maybe in a hospital bed, perhaps being operated on.

But no.

I'm not Vinnie.

And this isn't a hospital room.

I'm in Allie's body, one hand cuffed to a chain, which is linked to another pair of cuffs locked around a metal rail along the wall to my right.

This is Gavin's dungeon, and I am his prisoner.

I resist the urge to cry, scream, or make any sound at all. I have to assess the situation. The room is small, maybe ten by ten, so I can tell I'm alone, but I have no idea for how long, or what's beyond the door at the top of the stairs.

The dungeon is lit by a single lightbulb in the water-stained plaster ceiling. I think it has gray brick walls. There's a bed, a bucket for me to go to the bathroom in, and a sink with a roll of toilet paper and a plastic cup. That's it. No air vents, no windows, no escape.

I can't tell if it's day or night. There is only quiet.

I try to access Allie's memories to find out what's happened so far, what she remembers of being taken, if she has any idea where she is, or anything that might be of use. I get nothing, though. I can't even tell if anything's happened to her. Usually, when I'm in a host who has a recent traumatic experience, they leave a residual behind: memories, anxiety, even pain that weighs on me. But I'm getting nothing from Allie.

I try to sit up, but my head is still spinning.

Maybe she's been drugged the past two days?

I'm surprised, and a bit alarmed, that there's no gag on her mouth. He must have Allie somewhere nobody will hear her.

I'm wearing a T-shirt and jeans, which I suppose is a good sign. I could be naked and tied up. I've heard enough stories of girls and women being kept as sex slaves to know that's a very real possibility here. The fact that Allie is still dressed is a small comfort, but I can't extrapolate her future safety from that fact. Even if Gavin isn't a rapist — and let's not kid ourselves, he may very well be — we know he *is* a murderer. And Allie's seen his face. I can't think of a single reason he'd ever set her free.

Which means I need to either find a means of escape or persuade him to let her go.

I turn my head and examine the handcuff and rail along the wall. It's metal, gray, like one of those rails in a handicap stall. In fact, that's exactly what it looks like, which means the bastard must've installed this himself, for the sole purpose of confining someone. The scrape marks and dried blood tell me I'm right.

How many others have been in this room? And, more importantly, where are they now?

I continue examining the rail. There are two metal cups covering both spots where it's connected to the wall. Maybe if I can get them loose, I can find a way to slacken the screws. I press my hands against the wall, trying to determine if it is indeed brick. Sure feels like it, which means I won't be able to kick a hole to break free of the rail that way.

I wonder how Gavin managed to screw the rail into brick. Probably a drill with a heavy bit. My best bet seems to be pulling on the bar with both hands while pushing on the wall with my feet until I can loosen it — *if* I can loosen it — rather than unscrewing the rail.

But what then? There's still a door, and I can't imagine it's unlocked. Even if Gavin thinks I'm secure, he'd still bolt the door, right?

Maybe. Maybe not.

Indecision is a blade at my throat.

Should I try and break free now, make enough noise to draw my captor and suffer his wrath? I'm guessing he's a desperate man and would likely do anything to prevent Allie escaping and exposing him for the monster he is. Any attempt to flee while he's around would only push him into a corner. I need to bide my time, wait, see if he leaves, or maybe try and talk my way out of this.

This feels like the right solution, but I can't help wondering if he's out of the house now and that's why it's so quiet. This might be the perfect time to escape, and that's why I'm in Allie's body now.

Until recently, my jumps have felt random. But this feels like I'm part of some grand plan.

For four days I've been in the same town where Lara was killed and Allie was kidnapped. Being in Allie's body now *must* mean there's a connection here, at least among these four days. I'm not sure how Vinnie plays into it. Does he know Gavin? Or maybe he was there to give me the experience to fight? I can still feel his energy inside me, even though I'm no longer in his body.

And just like that, I remember him being shot, passing out, maybe even dying, and I suffer a wave of guilt.

I wonder if he's okay. And if so, what happened with the police, with his boss. He could be in a world of trouble right now, assuming he's alive, and a lot of that is my fault for opening the safe.

Stop, I tell myself, *you had no choice. It was that or be shot. You did the best you could.*

Besides, there's nothing I can do for him from here. It's time to focus on Allie and getting her the hell out of this sick bastard's dungeon.

Suddenly, movement outside the doorway. Somebody is fumbling with a sliding lock — so I *am* locked in.

I quickly lie back down, close my eyes, pretend I'm sleeping.

The door creaks open.

Footsteps echo in the small space as the human beast descends the stairs.

I risk opening my eyes.

And there he is, giving me his lunatic's smile.

"Good morning!" he says as if I'm a guest at his bed and breakfast and he's about to serve quiche.

I say nothing, guarded.

He stands in front of me, staring down.

"Still not happy to see me, eh? That'll change."

The hell it will!

I say nothing while he stares at me like a fat man

eyeballing cake. His creepy smile and delighted eyes make me want to vomit. Any thoughts I had about him *not* being a rapist are gone. He might not have raped Allie yet, but rape is lighting his eyes, for sure.

Having been in the bodies of a few people who have been raped, though, thankfully not during the crime, I know it's a pain, and often a shame, they carry for years, if not their entire lives. But it's not that aspect of the assault that scares me for Allie. It's something worse. Once you cross that line with someone you've kidnapped, you have no choice but to kill them. It's the only way Gavin can protect himself. Kill Allie, or keep her down here forever.

I can't let that happen.

I need to act.

I feel Vinnie's skills coursing through Allie's body. I have no idea if she can execute the same moves. After all, she doesn't have Vinnie's same physical build, his raw strength, or his training.

But *I* have the knowledge. And that, paired with my hate for Gavin, means we can do this. We can take him down.

Yeah, but look what happened to Vinnie. Even with all that skill, and even though you killed three assailants, you still managed to get him shot. He might even be dead!

I hush the fear inside me.

I can't let panic keep Allie a victim. I have to act.

I decide to engage Gavin.

"Why don't you let me go?" I ask, voice shaky.

"Why would I do that?"

"Because I don't think you meant to take me. I think I was in the wrong place at the wrong time. You didn't know what to do, so you grabbed me. Whatever was going on between you and Lara is none of my business. Just let me go, please. I promise I won't tell anyone anything about you. Hell, I don't even *know* anything about you!"

He stares at me for a long, uncomfortable moment. He appears to consider my request. Could it be that simple? Can I negotiate my way out of this?

"But I like you. Don't you like me?"

His grin tells me that he's not deranged enough to think I might like him. He's not some confused killer/kidnapper who thinks if he keeps the girl, she'll eventually grow to love him. No, he's clearly toying with me. He thinks he's better than me. He has no regard for life. I can see it in his eyes, just as I saw it through Lara's. This man is a psychopath.

I try to reason with him, anyway.

"I'm a kid," I say, hoping to disarm him. Yes, Allie is a teenager who may look to be of, or close to, the age of consent, but she's only fifteen, still a child. Maybe that will mean something to him.

He shakes his head, grinning. "Oh, don't play innocent with me."

"I'm fifteen! I'm not playing innocent. I *am* innocent. I haven't even kissed a boy!"

"Ooh, I've never had a virgin before. You'll be a nice change from all the whores. I promise I'll be gentle."

He reaches down to touch me, to touch Allie.

I act without thinking.

I grab his left arm with my right, then, with my fist balled up tight, drive my left hand, the chained one, up toward his neck, to deliver a lethal blow.

He turns, and my fist drives into his jaw instead. Painful, but hardly mortal.

He lets out a loud grunt then turns before I can make my next move, which would've been to wrap him with my legs and prevent him from getting away.

He grabs me by the neck, lifts me, and slams me against the wall.

The brick hits my head like a bat on a ball.

I WAKE.

The world is spinning. My head is pounding. I have no idea how long I've been out, but don't think it's been too long.

It was, however, long enough for Gavin to bind my hands with another pair of cuffs — *how many handcuffs does this asshole have?* — now linked to the chain attached to the rail.

He's standing over me. Jaw purple, eyes glaring. His grin is missing. There is no wicked delight in his eyes. He's pissed.

Good.

I'm too vulnerable to launch another attack but too proud to apologize or beg him not to hurt me.

"Try that again, and I'll bind your feet, too. You won't even be able to use the bucket."

"What do you want from me?" I ask, staring into his cold eyes.

He glares back, saying nothing.

"Is this what you were going to do to Lara? Kidnap her, bring her here so she could be your little pet or something?"

"No, she wasn't good enough to bring here."

The lack of emotion in his voice, and the casual way he dismisses Lara, makes me wish I had Vinnie's blade.

"So, what, I am?"

"You're probably not good enough, either," he says,

eyeing me up and down. "And I hadn't planned for you. I don't like to take a life until I know the life I'm taking."

I shake my head and say, "You're pathetic."

He smiles.

"Good. Keep it up. The more you fight, the more pleasure I'll have taking that fight out of you."

He turns toward the stairway.

"There's a sandwich on the sink. I suggest you eat it."

He ascends the steps, opens the door, then leaves.

I listen as he slides the lock shut.

I turn and look at the sandwich. I'm not sure if Allie has had anything to eat or drink yet, but judging from my growling stomach and dry mouth, I'd say it's been a while.

I sit up, head still swimming.

I stand, with just enough chain to reach the sink. As I look down at the sandwich, I notice that the waste bucket under the sink is empty. Has Allie not used it, or is Gavin dumping it each day?

I grab the sandwich and peel the bread apart to see peanut butter, no jelly. My stomach growls, and my mouth waters in anticipation.

I bite into the sandwich as if I haven't eaten in months.

I hope it's not poisoned, but figure if the asshole wanted me dead he's had any number of opportunities already. There's no need to trick me now.

I plow through the sandwich then turn on the sink, rinse the cup, fill it with cold water, and gulp it to empty.

I refill the cup and drink more. I set the cup back on the sink, then run water through my hands, over my face, and through my hair. The back of my head is tender, with a golf ball-sized lump. I gently touch it then pull my fingers back to see if there's blood. No.

I sit back on the bed even though I'm not in the mood to sit or lie. I want to be up, out of this room.

I look at the chain and the rail on the wall, wondering how much force it would take to yank the bar off. Can I do it without making so much noise that I draw his attention?

A thought occurs to me.

I haven't heard Gavin, except for when he's right outside my door. I'm guessing he has this place sound-proofed: he might not hear me if I start yanking on the rail.

Or, maybe he'll come right back in here and bind my hands and feet so that I can't even move. Or decide I'm too much of a pain in the ass and kill me to get things over with.

I lie back on the bed, weighing my options.

Now I'm feeling tipsy. And tired.

Did that bastard drug me?

I WAKE up to a pair of smacks on my cheek.

There is Gavin, above me. He's wearing a surgeon's mask, gloves, and gown. We're in another room, bright and all white. It looks like a doctor's office.

What the hell?

Startled, I try to move.

But I can't.

I'm naked, strapped to some sort of torture device, a cross between an exam table and a gynecologist's chair. My hands and arms are strapped to the table, and I'm leaned back at a 120-degree angle.

The worst part is that my legs are spread apart, also bound.

My heart is pounding, panic swarming in my skull, pushing me to get up, to fight back, to *somehow* escape before he does whatever sick thing he's about to do.

As if sensing my discomfort and vulnerability, Gavin walks around, assuming a position between my legs.

He stares down, his cheeks raising the surgeon's mask to betray his hidden smile.

I choke on my scream.

"Now, now, the more you resist, the harder this will be on you," he says in a faux-friendly voice.

What is he going to do?

He moves closer between my legs.

I feel his cold, gloved fingers squeeze my inner thighs.

My legs seize beneath his touch.

He leaves his fingers on my legs as if to taunt me, as if to say, *I can move them up any moment I choose, and there's nothing you can do.*

"Please!" I cry out, hating that I'm begging.

My words are garbled.

Tears stream from my eyes.

I can feel Allie's absolute terror as if she were right here with me, about to be violated in some way. And I would do anything to keep it from happening. I would say whatever I had to. I would step into my own body if I knew how, and take whatever horrors Gavin was about to visit upon her. Anything to spare her.

He squeezes my inner thighs tight, a cruel twist, fingers boring deep into my muscles.

I cry out.

I need to distract him.

I start pleading, urgently attempting to get the words out, hoping if I appear to be saying enough, his curiosity will overwhelm him, force him to remove the gag from my mouth.

My ploy works.

He comes over to me, fidgets with the straps, then pulls the ball from my mouth.

I gag on the taste and my own drool.

"What?" he asks impatiently, as if I'm keeping him from important work.

"Please, you don't have to do this. I don't know what happened to make you this way, but you don't have to do this."

His eyes look suddenly sad. I don't know if he's messing with me, or if he's seriously considering what I'm saying.

"Do you want to know what happened to me? What made me this way?" His eyes meet mine.

I fight the tears, open my eyes as wide as I can to show I'm listening.

"No, you don't care."

"Tell me."

He sets the ball gag aside and paces. "It all started when I was eleven."

I listen, but not because I care what made this man into the monster he is. He killed Lara. He kidnapped Allie. Whatever excuse he has will do nothing to dampen my white-hot hate. But I paint an accommodating expression onto my face, anyway.

"I grew up the son of a poor alcoholic who abused my sister and me. My mother never loved me. She saw me as a curse."

He covers his face with his hands, seeming to sob.

While I feel no sympathy for him, it's impossible to not feel something for a child in hell.

Then his sobs turn to laughing, and he removes his hands from his face. "You were buying that?"

My face is on fire. I glare at him, wishing I could break free of my restraints. I don't even need Vinnie's bladed buckle. I'll gouge his eyes with my fingers.

Just give me a chance.

He turns to me and smiles. "I'm sorry. I just hate hearing people's sob stories of why they're so fucked up. I have no idea why I am the way I am. I had a rich father and a loving mother. What more could a child want?"

I continue glaring at him.

He crosses his arms.

"Oh, come on, lighten up, or neither one of us will have a good time."

He turns to the counter and sink, his back to me, doing something I can't see. Then he turns around, holding a scalpel in his gloved hands.

He walks toward me, slowly, deliberately, milking the terror in my eyes.

"Help! Help!"

He raises his hands as if conducting an orchestra. "Scream all you want. Nobody will hear you. No one can save you."

He continues toward me.

I scream louder, shaking in a vain attempt to break free from the restraints.

He stops beside my face, looks down, tracing the scalpel against my breast.

A cold chill runs through me.

I whimper, "Please, don't."

His hand stops.

He's staring into my eyes.

I don't know if he's messing with me again, but something has him spooked.

He shakes his head.

"No, it can't be."

"Can't be what?" I ask, sure there's a punchline coming. The minute I fall for his joke, he'll sink the blade into me.

"I killed you. Twice."

And now I'm the one frozen.

He can see through me, can see the me that is in here, just as he had seemed to see me in Lara.

I don't know what to say. Words leave my mouth anyway.

"Yes, it is me. And I'll keep coming back to haunt you. Every time you kill me, I'll come back, until I get what I want."

He shakes his head, slowly, whispering, "No, no, no."

Then he screams, violently shaking his head.

He returns to the counter.

My heart races, unsure of what to expect. Will he set me free? Or is he getting another instrument to finish me quicker?

He turns around, a hypodermic in his hand.

He rushes forward.

I cry out, "No!"

He injects whatever it is into my neck then turns and runs from the room.

Whatever he put in me is acting quickly. So quickly, I —

I don't remember passing out.

I wake up back in the dungeon, chained to the rail.

My head is fuzzy, again, as I try to make sense of what happened. But I can barely remember. My head is stuffed with memories that aren't mine, or Allie's. Instead, I have bits of Vinnie and Yvonne bouncing around my head, but not the memories I experienced while trapped in their bodies. Bits of their pasts are jumbled with my present.

Everything feels so confusing.

Is this some effect of whatever drug Gavin injected me with?

If so, how is it affecting *my* mind?

It's not like my physical self, or my brain in particular, jumped into Allie's body. Yet it's as if it has. Like I've somehow collected these people's memories and carried them with me into Allie's shell, and now the drugs are causing them to flood my senses.

I try to focus on the present, the room I'm in, this current body, as some way to anchor myself. If I don't, I'm afraid the memories will carry me off into madness. And maybe bring Allie along.

I focus on the ceiling light.

I don't want to fall asleep.

I want to stay in this body.

I need to stay with Allie, to protect her.

It's an incandescent bulb, clear, small dark spot on the tip, glass stem, tungsten filament, bright burning yellow light.

I focus on that light.

If I could only harness the light in some way, use it to transport us both away from this dungeon.

Chapter Five

WEDNESDAY

~

I'M AWAKE.

I'm no longer in Allie.

And I'm not in Bay Cove. I'm in Las Orillas, California.

I'm in the body of a forty-one-year-old black man named Charles Tompkins. Someone moves beneath the sheets beside me. I turn to see Charles's boyfriend, Danny, smiling up at me in the soft blue glow of light bleeding through the bedroom curtains. He's not just white, but maybe the palest man I've ever seen, with blue eyes, and shoulder-length red hair. Despite his trim goatee, Danny has delicate, feminine features, which I find attractive even though I believe my true soul belongs to a straight male.

Gender and sex are fluid for me. I tend to absorb my host's feelings when it comes to these things, which I suppose makes my job a lot easier. To have no feelings or attraction to the person I'm forced to be with for a day or so would make things so much more difficult.

"Well, you're up early," Danny says. "I guess you *are* excited about today?"

I have no idea what he means.

I have a feeling that Danny is teasing me, so I nod and shrug.

He says, "I promise, it's not going to be that bad."

"*That bad?* So, in other words, it's going to be at least a *little bad?*"

"She changed my life. And I'm sure she'll do the same for you."

I search Charles's memories for a clue, but I don't see much. An overload of leftovers from Vinnie, Yvonne, and now Allie still runs through my head. I've never carried so many memories before, and I'm getting scared.

It's tough enough to do this thing I do — this body jumping — under normal circumstances. But now carrying their thoughts and fears with me into the next body makes it nearly impossible to focus on the memories of my host. Add to that my fear for Allie's well-being and trying to figure out how Charles fits into any of this, and my current state is a chaotic mess.

And being out of Washington scares me. Does this mean I can no longer help Allie? Did I blow my chance, and now I'm back to jumping into randoms without any connection to Allie?

Danny hits me on the shoulder. "Right?"

"Right what?" I ask, only now aware that he was talking while I tuned him out.

"Hello? Earth to Charles. You want to do this, right? If you think it's stupid and you're only doing it for me, please, don't do me any favors."

I still don't know what he's going on about. I do my

best with what I have. "No, I want to do this. Really. Just thinking about a dream I had."

Danny sits up in bed, wraps an arm around me, and pulls me back to lie beside him. "What did you dream about?" He circles his fingers in my chest hair.

A flash of memory informs me that Danny is very much into analyzing dreams. Charles, not so much. He tends to see dreams as the body's way of processing memories. Nothing to examine, no tea leaves to read. But Charles usually humors him and tells him his dreams, anyway.

From what I can tell, these two couldn't be more different. Charles is a copywriter, straight-laced, and rather conservative. Danny, five years younger, is a carefree art teacher, with a mystical bent, evidenced by the plethora of crystals hanging from the dresser mirror, and the long row of psychic-themed books lined up on the headboard's built-in bookshelf. He also partakes of various recreational drugs while Charles will barely drink more than a glass of wine with dinner. Somehow, they've made their relationship work for more than two years.

"Go on," Danny says, smiling, "You always have the weirdest dreams." This is a compliment coming from him. I can tell that he uses these little sessions to loosen Charles, coaxing him to enjoy the moment and embrace the unknown.

In other words, pull the stick from his ass.

I'm not sure why, if I'm agitated with Danny's inquiries, or annoyed at being stuck in this body rather than being in someone who can help Allie, I decide to tell him something *really* weird.

"I dreamed I was stuck in these other people's bodies. Every day or so, I'd wake up in someone else, and I kept jumping around from body to body for almost a year."

"Really?" he asks, eyebrows arched.

"Yes. And my last body was a teenage girl who'd been abducted by a serial killer. He had her in a dungeon, tied to some chair, and was going to perform some sick ritual or experiment or something on her."

Danny stares at me with no expression.

I worry that maybe I said too much, something that gave away the truth.

"So," I ask, "what do you think that means?"

I'm smiling inside, like the petulant toddler who throws his plate on the floor when he isn't getting his way, to rock the boat and see how his parents deal with *that*.

"Wait, wait, I think I have an idea." Danny sits up in bed, his eyes alight like he is about to solve a puzzle he's been working for years.

I sit up beside him as if he might illuminate the enigma *I've* been working on, too.

"Okay, here's what I think. I think you waking up in different bodies is a dream manifestation of your need to be all these different things to different people. Maybe it's also because you're still in the closet to your family and some of your oldest friends."

I can sense that this is an old discussion, something that Danny has tried to move Charles on many times. I suppose I could do an eye roll or something to indicate impatience with his interpretation's direction, but I'm curious to hear more, so I hold his eyes to mine.

"I think the girl represents your soul. Your authentic self, and the more you have to hide in these various guises, the more you're killing your authentic self. It's something you're barely aware of on a conscious level, but your subconscious sees it, and is trying to tell you to stop living a lie, to be yourself, with everyone in your life."

Danny rests his hands on his lap, looking at me with expectant eyes. "Well? Does that sound right to you?"

"It sounds more like psychoanalyzing than dream interpretation."

"Sometimes, they're one and the same."

"Maybe, but that doesn't mean I'm going to tell the world that I'm gay because of some dream."

"Hey, I don't want to tell you what to do. I'm just saying that maybe hiding this part of yourself is bothering you a lot more than you realize. You're creating a cognitive dissonance, which is manifesting itself in depression and bad dreams."

I don't know what to say. I can't deny that Charles is depressed since I have no idea. This isn't *my* argument to have, nor my decision to come out. It's Charles's. While I agree with Danny that people can't truly be happy while living according to the rules and expectations of others, Charles must have his reasons for not coming out. While it might make him happier in the long run for me to act on his behalf and leave the closet for him, I can't be cavalier with someone's life enough to force them.

"I don't want to talk about this."

"Fine," Danny huffs. "Okay, I'm gonna get ready for school."

Danny showers and I head to their shared office. There's a large psychedelic print on the wall of two see-through people engaged in a kiss with all sorts of vibrant lights swirling behind them and through them. Charles's memory tells me it's an Alex Gray print that Charles bought for Danny last Christmas.

I turn on the computer and start searching for information, first on Allie. I scan some stories, none of them offering anything new. Then I find a video posted this morning from a Washington news station.

I hope for good news.

The video begins by showing a bunch of people combing nearby woods in the dark, searching for Allie. I hope they've found her, and that's why this is news. Maybe Gavin had second thoughts after seeing me — if it was me he saw — in Allie.

The video switches to a picture of Lara Spencer. A grave reporter talks about how the sheriff's department believes the death of Lara Spencer and Allie's disappearance are likely related.

Then the video switches to a reporter standing with someone it takes me a moment to recognize.

I stare in disbelief at the name beneath the woman, Maryanne Martin — Allie's mother. This is *not* the person I knew. She's made up, hair quaffed and colored a less toxic shade of blonde, wearing nice clothes. Nothing at all like the woman who eyed me from her doorway: the puffy-faced, trashy alcoholic with torn clothes and a rat's nest of hair.

Anger courses through me as I listen to her talking about how much she misses her daughter, and how she's praying that the "Good Lord will bring her home soon."

"Liar," I say to the screen.

"Liar?" Danny is standing behind me in his towel.

I turn, surprised he's out of the shower so quickly.

"Yeah," I say, fumbling for an excuse, "she doesn't look like she gives a damn about her daughter."

Danny leans on the chair behind me, looking over me at the computer screen. "Oh, this is that missing girl in Washington?"

"Yeah," I say, surprised that Danny knows the case. But then I figure it *is* a missing pretty white girl, and add to that the dead pretty white woman, and you have national news.

Given another month, you'll have three Lifetime movies of the week.

"Yeah, her mother looks shifty to me, too."

I smile. Danny has a good feel for people.

"You think she did it?" he asks.

"What? Kidnapped her daughter?"

"No, maybe she found out the dead woman was having an affair with her daughter then went to break it up and wound up killing them both."

"Really?" I laugh. "*That's* what you think happened?"

So much for Danny having a good feel for people.

"I dunno. Nothing surprises me these days. And that mother looks like she's guilty of *something.*"

"Probably, but I don't think she's a killer. Just a piece of shit mother."

Danny laughs. "Maybe this news story is why you're dreaming of being an abducted teenage girl."

I'm not sure if he's really suggesting that the dream could be a random memory misinterpreted, as Charles suspects they are, or if this is Danny's way of backing down from the earlier escalation. Maybe this is how they avoid getting into bigger fights, broaching subjects with tact then backing away once a line's been crossed.

"Maybe," I say, figuring I don't want to send him off to work all bummed out about our discussion.

Danny heads back to the bedroom to get dressed.

As he finishes getting ready for school, I watch the end of the report to see that Allie is still missing, then search for information on Vinnie.

I find an article on the *Chronicle's* website about the shootings at the club. It isn't until the end of the story that I see Vinnie listed as a club worker who is still in intensive care at the hospital. That's it: a single sentence.

A man's life reduced to thirteen words.

I click off the article and pull up the most recent document in Charles's folder marked *Client Work* and pretend to work until Danny is dressed and ready to head out the door.

I walk him to the garage and kiss him goodbye.

"Remember, at six o' clock we're going to Madam Monique."

I nod, having no idea who the hell Madam Monique is. My first impression, from the name, is that she runs some kind of sex club or something. Then I remember all the psychic-themed books lined in a row.

Is he taking me to see a freaking psychic?

This is going to be a long-ass day.

We say goodbye, and I head back into the office to look up Madam Monique. Her website is sparse — a black screen with her name, address, phone number, an image of tarot cards, and a note at the bottom:

Call for rates and to schedule an appointment to change your life.

Call for rates, eh? Is that so she can determine how much you're worth and how much to milk you for? I have about as much patience for *psychics* as I do televangelists and other charlatans exploiting the desperate. I'm rather surprised by my strong reaction to the idea of seeing a psychic. I wonder if I'd ever crossed paths with one in my life before this body jumping, or if I'm drawing on memories from other hosts I've been in before. Over time, my memories of time spent inside a host always fade. Reminders gnarl in a giant ball that's impossible to untangle. That's probably good considering how difficult it's been managing memories from Lara, Vinnie, and Allie.

I keep searching for information, whatever I can find on any or all of my last three hosts.

Finding nothing but variations on the same regurgitated stories, I end up sitting in front of the computer, staring at the screen, numb.

I SPEND the rest of the day stabbing at Charles's client work. Fortunately, he's well organized and ahead of schedule, so there's not too much I *need* to do. I do some light copyediting, but don't want to write new content. I'm guessing he'd notice new words when he returns to his body, and wonder who the hell wrote them.

DANNY COMES home at 5:20.

I greet him with a kiss, dressed and ready to see the psychic. He drives, while I try accessing Charles's memories to see why we're going. But like the rest of the day before now, I can't find anything. I don't want to ask, as I'm sure the reason is important to Danny, and if *Charles* has forgotten, it might injure him or their relationship. Like forgetting a birthday or something.

When I picture a psychic's shop, I imagine a mysterious ancient building tucked away in a dark wooded area. A handful of creepy decorations outside, crystal balls, totems, or other supernatural items to create a specific strain of atmosphere.

Madam Monique's shop couldn't defy my expectations more. It's located in a relatively new and upscale-looking town center offering all the latest trends: overpriced faux-French furniture, eclectic clothes, foodie havens, and esoteric boutiques.

Her shop is tucked between an *artisan* ice cream parlor and a shop called Berceuse Lullaby with lifelike child mannequins in the window frozen mid-frolic in fashionable clothes. The kids look eerily dead, like some psycho child killer's staging of a crime scene, but hey, what do I know?

Madam Monique's windows aren't painted black or covered in drapes like I imagined. They're large and open, revealing a small, modern shop that could easily belong to a realtor.

I find myself disappointed that there's no attempt at atmosphere. I don't know if this makes the Madam more or less suspect.

We go inside.

The front part of the shop is empty save for a few chairs gathered around a coffee table with magazines to approximate a small waiting room. There's a front counter, and behind that, a door, which I imagine leads to the real show.

A young black woman stands behind the counter, wearing trendy clothes and a hipster hat. "Hello, Danny," she says, smiling as she looks from him to me. "And this must be Charles."

She reaches out to shake my hand.

I shake it.

"I've heard so much about you."

I don't know who she is, so I can't exactly say the same thing. Is she a receptionist, or Madam Monique herself?

"This is Staci," Danny says, relieving my confusion.

"Hi, Staci," I say.

"So, are you ready for your first reading?"

So *that's* what's going on. I don't know why I would've expected something other than a reading; why else would you go to a psychic? But for some reason, I hadn't put two with two for the obvious answer.

I nod, unable to hide my nervous grin.

"It's okay," Staci says, "you're not the first skeptic or the last. But I have a feeling you'll change your tune once she talks with you."

"I'll try and be open-minded." It's an absolute lie. I'm already contemplating the ways which this "reading" will be rigged. Will she pretend to know things about me, when, in fact, Danny unwittingly supplied her with plenty of information?

I look over at Danny, grinning like an eager puppy, or maybe a *dumb rube*.

He's so excited for me to experience this thing that's changed him, I feel kind of guilty. He's not sharing this with Charles, but with *me*. While I can sense Charles's skepticism, perhaps he was a bit more open or at least pretending to be for Danny. And worse, Charles will likely have no recollection of this event, which means no matter what happens, I'm robbing this couple of an important memory — one that could be foundation building, or decaying.

But it's too late to try and get out of this now.

Staci says, "Come on, she's waiting."

Danny grabs my hand and leads me back into Madam Monique's lair.

The back of the shop delivers what I was expecting — new age music, enough lit candles to fill a cathedral, sweet burning incense. Dark purples, reds, and black fabrics drape the walls, and ebony shelves are lined with crystals, dream catchers, and statues. The main attraction sits in the middle of the room — a black medium-sized circular table with a large crystal ball, tarot cards, totems that mean nothing to me. Five seats surround it.

And then there is Monique.

She is an old black woman wearing long flowing silks

and a blue scarf around her long, surprisingly dark dreads. She's at least eighty, maybe much older. I wonder if her age lends to her authenticity with the locals.

Her eyes are closed.

I'm not sure if she's nodded off or if this is her attempt at drama.

I look at Danny. He's looking at Monique like she's a maternal figure in his life. Maybe she is. From the scant memories I've seen, he's led a difficult life until recently. He's happy now. I wonder if it's because of his relationship with Charles, or some *revelation* reached by Madam Monique.

His happy look sours my stomach. I don't want this woman to be a fake, but how could she be anything but? I won't go so far as to say that the world has no genuine clairvoyants — my existence is proof of unexplainable phenomena — but there is no way even a hundredth of the so-called psychics out there looking to charge you for their *spiritual guidance* are genuine. The odds are damn strong that Madam Monique is another charlatan robbing an innocent rube and telling him what he wants to hear.

I hate her.

Staci invites us to sit down then leaves the room, quietly closing the door behind her.

Danny sits beside the woman.

He motions for me to sit on her other side, leaving two chairs empty. I don't want to sit that close to Madam Monique, but do as instructed.

Her hands are folded in her lap, and she still has her eyes closed. I'm weary of the act already. I'm tempted to say, "Hello!" nice and loud, with no social grace whatsoever.

But I remain quiet, respectful for Danny.

She opens her eyes.

She looks at Danny and smiles. "Danny," she says warmly.

She turns to me, and for a second I see her smile falter. Even at only a flash I recognize what it is — a look of judgment.

Does she disapprove of my relationship with Danny because I'm black and he's white? I can see in Charles's memories how some of his older relatives had treated him when he went out with white girls, back when he was still trying to convince himself he wasn't gay.

Maybe she's not prejudiced. Maybe she recognizes me as a skeptic. She sees that pulling the wool over my eyes won't be as easy as it was with poor, sweet Danny.

No, ma'am, the gravy train has come to its final stop. You'll not be exploiting Danny any longer. Not after I expose you for what you are.

In the space of that look I've gone from wanting to maintain Danny's illusion to hoping I can break it. I feel compelled to protect him. He's not *my* lover, but I have feelings for him just the same. An urge to watch over him and protect him from predators like this.

"And you must be Charles?"

"Yes," I say smiling as if to say, *I've got your card, Sister.*

"Danny says that you'd like a reading?"

"Yes, ma'am."

"Okay, then. Let us all hold hands, shall we?"

I look at Danny, still grinning like a naive idiot who thinks this woman is about to convince me. Convince me of *what*, I'm not sure. Why Charles needs to believe in this mystical stuff, I don't know. But he has so much hope in his eyes.

Danny takes the madam's hand.

I reach out and take Danny's, warm to the touch.

Then I take Madam's.

A spark of static electricity jumps between us.

I snap my hand back, embarrassed at how much it hurt, but trying not to make too big of a deal.

Madam Monique laughs. "Ah, you've got a live wire here."

Danny laughs.

She holds out her hand again for me to take.

Again, she closes her eyes.

She starts mumbling something. I'm not sure if it's in another language, or gibberish, or maybe some variation of "Oh, what fools we have with us today. Please, Almighty Dollar, help me separate them from their funds in the most momentous of ways."

I look at Danny to find that he's closing his eyes, too. Is this some kind of prayer circle?

I keep my eyes open. If we're going to do a seance or summon spirits, or some other nonsense, I want to see the strings moving furniture around.

A long silence follows the mumbling. Danny's eyes are still closed. It all feels ritualized. I wonder if other psychics do things this way or if this is Madam Monique's personal brand of crazy.

"All right," she says, opening her eyes, "we may begin."

Madam Monique looks down at the tarot cards as if she's considering a reading, but then her hands move toward the crystal ball as if drawn by magnets. She moves her hands over the glass in practiced, fluid motions, fingers gliding a hair from the surface. It's hard not to be mesmerized by her showmanship.

I watch the ball, not sure what to expect. Will it glow? Will it fill with smoke? It's completely clear, and to me, looks like an ordinary glass globe supported by a fancy black and gold stand.

She's looking into the ball, lips twitching as she mumbles.

I look up at Danny. His eyes are on the ball, entranced.

"You are at a crossroads," she says.

I chuckle inside. Just the sort of vague statement that anyone can interpret to mean more than the madam is saying. I wonder if this is the type of mystical wisdom that has fooled Danny into thinking she was the real deal. So far, I'm not impressed.

"You're tormented over your choices. Unsure of what to do."

Again, that could be true of anyone. I look at Danny. He's looking at me, likely trying to gauge whether I'm convinced.

A suspicion crosses my mind. I wonder if Danny and the *psychic* are in on this together. Maybe he told her that he wanted me to come out, so she said, "Bring him here; I'll convince him."

I meet Danny's eyes, searching for any sign of his duplicity. He looks too sweet, too naive, to ever lie to me like that.

I look back down at the ball, waiting for Madam to say something else.

"Oh," she says, her face twisting as if she's seen something she wishes she hadn't.

Ah, here comes the part where she reels me in with some artificial vision.

Her face continues to contort, her hands now on the ball as if stuck. Danny is looking at her, brow knotted in confusion, or maybe in concern. This isn't part of the usual show.

"So much blood," she says.

I swallow, sure I didn't hear what I think I heard.

I wonder if I should interrupt. Danny must be reading

my mind, as he gives me a look telling me to hold tight.

"Allie needs you."

I feel as if someone has hit me in the chest, hard enough to stop my heart. I stare at Madam Monique as she turns to me.

Her eyes widen.

"You're not Charles. Why are you here?"

She looks terrified, hands now off the ball, arms crossing her chest as if ready to defend against an attack, from me.

"What?" Danny asks.

"Huh?" She raises a hand to her head. "Oh … I'm sorry. I'm not feeling well. Can we reschedule?"

I'm not ready to leave. "What did you see?"

She starts to get up, eager to get as far away from me as possible.

I can't let her go. There's no way this can be a coincidence. She sees that I'm not Charles. She *saw* Allie. She *saw* the blood.

I grab her arm.

Her head snaps up, eyes wide on me, shocked by my touch.

She pulls back, nearly falling over, pushing herself back from the table and toward a door behind the room.

"Are you okay?" Danny asks, his face wracked with confusion, his eyes darting between Madam and me.

"Yes, yes, I just need to rest. Please, reschedule with …" She seems to forget her assistant's name. "Get with Staci, and reschedule."

She rushes through the door, closes it behind her. I hear the deadbolt turning.

I go to the door, bang on it. "Please, Madam, I need answers."

She doesn't respond.

I bang again.

"Charles!" Danny grabs my arm and pulls me away from the door.

I ignore him.

"Madam, please. I need to know what you saw."

Still no response.

The door behind us opens. Staci is standing there.

"What's going on?"

"I don't know," Danny tells her. "She said some weird things, then that her head hurt. She asked us to go."

"I think she saw something in my future that scared her," I say, manufacturing a lie to explain my urgency. I can't come right out and ask how she knows I'm not Charles. But I can pretend that I'm scared by her glimpse of my future. "I need to know what she saw."

"Madam wasn't feeling good this morning." Staci gives us a polite smile. "I'm sorry. Just call me, and we'll reschedule, for free."

But I don't want to leave. I *can't* reschedule. I'm sure I won't be here tomorrow.

"Come on," Danny says, tugging on my arm.

Judging from the way he's looking at me, my assertiveness is out of character. I need to walk away, reconsider my options.

"I'm sorry," I say, "of course. Let's reschedule. The sooner, the better."

"I'll call you later, Daniel. Right now, I need to tend to Madam."

"Of course," Danny says. "Tell her we hope she's feeling better."

We leave.

Our walk to the car is quiet. So is the ride home.

Halfway to our apartment, Danny asks, "Who is Allie?"

"I don't know," I lie.

Danny is quiet. I don't think he believes me.

I'm not sure what to say, so every thought stays inside me. I'm trying to suss things out in my head. What did she see? Did she see what happened with Lara or Vinnie? Or did she see something in the future, or maybe happening *to* Allie right now?

So much blood. Allie needs you.

Could she have seen Allie's blood? Is that monster hurting her now? Or is it something he's going to do? Can Madam Monique see the future? She certainly saw Allie's name and said I wasn't Charles. I can hardly believe it, but she *is* the real deal. And I *need* to talk to her again.

Danny is quiet as he drives, his wheels turning.

"Why did she say you're not Charles?"

"I don't know why she said any of that crazy stuff," I say, desperate for Danny to believe me. "The thing about blood? That name? None of it makes any sense."

"Do you *know* an Allie?"

I see fear on his face. Maybe he thinks I'm cheating on him, or perhaps that Allie is some old flame I'm still thinking of.

I shake my head. "No … I don't think so."

"Allie Martin."

I pretend not to remember the name. "Who?"

"The missing girl in Washington. Her name is Allie Martin."

"Yeah, but what could that have to do with me?" I say, hoping he doesn't think I'm involved in a kidnapping, hoping that Charles hadn't recently disappeared for a few days, or taken a trip to Washington.

A horrifying thought hits me like a hammer. What if Charles *is* somehow involved? What if *that* is his connection to everything, and *why* I'm in his body?

No. That theory doesn't feel right at all.

Danny is thinking about something. As we pull into our driveway, he finally says it.

"Your dream about that abducted girl. Do you think you were dreaming about Allie? That you're somehow connected?"

I stare out the window, at our apartment, and I wonder if I should tell Danny everything. I've wanted someone to confide in for so long, to unburden myself, to get honest advice, to hear someone else's theories on what might be happening to me. I've lived hundreds of lives, and have been around thousands of different people, and yet I might be the planet's loneliest soul. I look into Danny's trusting blue eyes, and feel like I could tell him anything. Surely, he'd understand, and have the perfect words to say.

But I swore to myself long ago that I'd never share this secret. It isn't fair to anyone. It might help me to talk, but this is *my* burden to bear. If I tell Danny, he'll never see Charles the same way again.

He'd think his lover was crazy, and even crazier the next day or so when Charles returns to his body, denying ever having spouted such nonsense. That's a kind of crazy you can never totally trust. Danny would never feel safe wondering when Charles might *snap* again.

Even if Danny *did* believe my story, how could he ever trust his boyfriend, or anyone, ever again, with the knowledge that at any moment a stranger might be pretending to be his lover, friend, or coworker?

I long to tell him, but can't do that to Danny.

He asks again, "Do you think you're somehow connected to her?"

"I don't know. I don't even know how that would be possible?"

Danny kills the engine but makes no effort to leave the

car. He's still thinking.

"I've got a theory."

"Shoot."

"You know about the collective unconscious, right?"

"More or less."

"Well, maybe this is one of those things. Consider this. Everything is energy. Our bodies. Our thoughts, all energy. And there are certain people who can pick up on others' energies. So maybe you're somehow picking up on thoughts that Allie is putting out there?"

"So, I'm picking up her psychic signal?"

Danny's eyebrows are raised, his voice faster, like he's chasing a revelation.

"It's not as crazy as you might think."

"I didn't say anything."

"Yeah, but I know you. You're skeptical."

"Yes, but I'm not so closed-minded that I won't consider possibilities."

"Maybe it's not that. Maybe it's something else. Are you familiar with quantum entanglement?"

"Not exactly an expert," I say.

"Me either, just in the broadest sense. But the theory is that every particle has an opposite or connected particle. Like mirror images. If you separate them, they'll still act as if they're together. There are scientific experiments that more or less prove the theory, two particles responding to light, even though only one is exposed. Maybe you're somehow connected to Allie, and sensing what's happening to her?"

His theory might be off target, but I wonder if it explains my circumstances in some way. It could account for some things, though it falls apart once you consider how many people I'm connected to.

"You think maybe Madam Monique saw these

connections?"

Danny nods.

"Here's the question," I say, grateful for an opportunity to discuss this without revealing the truth, "do you think she saw something that already happened, is happening now or is going to happen?"

Danny looks like he needs a joint to break this idea down and explore it from every possible angle.

I press on. "Has she told you about things in your past, present, or future?"

"A bit of all."

"And was she accurate about any of it?"

"*All of it.*"

I stare. It isn't the answer I want to hear.

"I need to talk to her again."

"I'll call her later," Danny says. "Maybe we can schedule something for tomorrow."

"No, I need to talk to her tonight."

"I don't think that's gonna happen. She seemed pretty shook up."

"Can you call? Just see."

Danny says okay then makes the call.

I wait, patiently.

Nobody answers.

Danny leaves a message, asking Staci to please call us back.

He hangs up.

I want to ask him to drive back there, now, but I know he'll argue. I can't go back in the apartment and do nothing. Maybe going out to dinner will give us an excuse to drive back by Madam Monique's. I try and remember the name of the steak house I saw in the town center.

"Hey, what was that steak house we drove by near Madam's?"

"Juno's?"

"Yeah," I say, "want to go there for dinner?"

He looks at me suspiciously. "You're not going to ask me to drive back to Madam's, are you?"

"Only if they don't call us back."

"You're really worked up about this, aren't you?"

I'm not sure if he's about to tease me and the fact that I'm now a believer, or if he's concerned. Maybe both.

"I'll admit that she scared me."

Danny hugs me. "It'll be okay."

I hug him back, wishing I could tell him more, but knowing I can't.

DINNER IS GOOD, even though I'm anxiously awaiting Staci's call. When we don't hear back, I convince Danny to swing by Madam Monique's.

Her lights are off.

I get out of the car and knock on the door anyway.

No response.

This will have to wait until tomorrow. But will I be here?

AT BEDTIME, Danny is in the mood.

Fortunately, I'm able to convince him that I have a headache, and suggest we smoke a few bowls instead.

We discuss his theories in bed, but nothing seems to approach the possible truth in his original ideas.

As I feel sleep coming, I hope to stay in Charles for at least one more day. Just long enough to talk to Madam Monique again.

Chapter Six

~

I WAKE UP. I am no longer Charles, though due to a splitting headache and foggy thoughts, I don't yet know whose body I'm in.

I'm not sure why, but it seems like I tend to wake too often in people who spent the night partying like there was no tomorrow. It amazes me how careless people can be with their bodies, from overeating to drug and alcohol abuse, people take their vessels for granted, as if they don't need to care for the very thing which should carry them into old age. Most hosts I've been inside treat their cars better than their bodies.

I sit up, looking around the apartment.

It's small and dark. There are beer bottles everywhere.

There's a bottle of painkillers on the nightstand, lying empty on its side.

Did my host take all those last night? Is this a normal

routine, or is he *trying* to kill himself? I feel an overwhelming sense of pain and guilt, even though I have no associated memories to explain the emotions.

I get out of bed, legs shaky, body aching.

The thin sliver of light coming through the windows grates on my frayed nerves. A part of me wants to crawl back into bed, to ride this wretchedness out. But I have a feeling if I do that, my host might not wake back up.

My stomach lurches.

I stumble toward the bathroom, barely make it to the toilet, drop to my knees, then vomit into the porcelain bowl.

I sit there retching for what feels like forever, as if releasing toxins from every pore.

I finally stand.

I don't know how long ago my host went to sleep or took those pills, but I feel like if I hadn't come along and woken him, he'd be dead now.

I stand up, flick on the lights, and stare into the bathroom mirror, hoping that will jar some of the host's memories into my brain. At least give me a name to work with.

But I don't need memories.

I recognize the host.

His name is Thomas (Tommy) Clarke, one of the two reporters at the *Bay Cove Chronicle*.

He's twenty-eight, just under six feet tall, and looks like someone you'd see in a Starbucks dutifully writing in their Moleskine journal. He has thick shoulder-length brown hair, coffee-colored eyes, and a beard that looks somewhere between hipster and lumberjack. He usually wears thick black-framed glasses, though he only needs them to see far. In my prior hosts' memories, I see him as a hard worker, one of the first to arrive, and last to leave at the office, always offering to help others in the newsroom. A nice, decent guy.

I look in the mirror and ask, "What the hell happened to you?"

His memories are still refusing me, which might be the first time it's taken so long to download, for lack of a better term, the *necessary past* from a host.

Did alcohol and drugs stall the machinery?

I head back into Tommy's bedroom, searching for something that might jar a few memories free. The room is small. He has a trunk where he keeps his clothes; an overflowing bookshelf: lots of sci-fi, books on writing, a few tomes of literary fiction, books by journalists, and a wide array of biographies.

There are also several journals. I'm not sure if they're novels or diaries. I don't want to pick any up yet, as I prefer to keep the process of discovering my host pure.

I turn to his desk. He has a small iMac, tons of folders and papers covering his desk, which I think are probably work related. There's a cork board behind his iMac with a lot of little yellow notes, index cards with contact info, and a single photograph.

I look at the photo.

It's a picture of him and Lara sitting at a restaurant, cozy in a booth, both of them smiling for the camera, holding up drinks. Were they close friends? Or had they once been more? I remember Yvonne's comment to Lara, how she could always go out with Tommy if things with Gavin didn't work out. Maybe there *is* a history here.

They look so happy in the picture. I get a weird sensation, as if I'm peering into my own past.

My mind flashes, and suddenly I'm *in* that memory — from both sides. They were at a late night dinner with Yvonne, when she suddenly had to take care of something back at the office, leaving Tommy and Lara alone for a good half hour.

Tension had been building for some time, that thing where you both wonder if maybe there's something more than friendship bubbling under the surface. They both felt it.

As Lara, I'm laughing, having a good time, wondering if Tommy likes me in that way. He seems like he does, but has yet to *act*. I consider making the first move, but I'm coming off a bad relationship and don't want to lose one of my few friends, let alone ruin our small office dynamic. I like my job, a lot, and don't need a reason to hate it.

Then I experience the same night through Tommy's memories.

I'm nervous, and a little mad at Yvonne, who had threatened to do this if I didn't finally make a move on Lara. She left us alone on purpose, trying to set us up. But I'm getting mixed signals.

I've never had a relationship that lasted more than a few weeks. I'm insecure, had a shitty childhood with parents who criticized my every move. I was an only child, and couldn't help but think they never wanted me to begin with. They wanted an adult, someone they could manage, someone who didn't demand things like time and attention, neither of which they had much to give. I've never felt confident of my place with people, so I bury myself in work. It's easier this way. I'm good at my job, and know how to do it better than those reporters at the *Daily*. It's one of the few things I'm not just confident in, but can be cocky about.

But when it comes to relationships, I turn stupid. I'm insecure and needy, always screwing things up. I don't mean to, but it's happened enough times to know it'll probably happen again.

And Lara is too nice of a girl to do that to.

I love talking to her, and not just about the job and local politics, but about things like books and movies and music. I love listening to her going on and on about art. I could spend days lost in conversation with her. And that says nothing of the days I could spend kissing her, touching her, making love to her. She's the closest to a perfect match for me I'd ever known, but also a good friend.

And I don't want to screw that up.

Too scared to make a move, I do nothing.

When Yvonne comes back, she gives me a look as if to ask, "Well, did you do anything?"

I shrug.

She mouths the word, *Idiot.*

And of course she's right.

Back to the present.

I stare at the photo on the cork board and feel overwhelmed by the crushing loss. The bitter regret Tommy was trying to drown.

I look around at the beer bottles, the pills. He *was* trying to kill himself. I'm still missing his memories, but it makes perfect sense.

I go to his computer and turn it on.

The screen asks for a password.

But nothing comes.

Dammit.

I try *Lara.*

Nothing.

I stop. I'm not sure if he has a script that will lock me out or wipe the data if I keep entering incorrect guesses. I'll have to wait for him to supply the answer.

I decide to shower.

The water feels good — like it's washing away some of my excess baggage. Even if it's not erasing memories from the past few days, it's at least rinsing some of the anxiety that's been building inside me.

After I wash up and get dressed, I open the curtains and clean his apartment. The living room and kitchen aren't in terrible shape. It's mostly the bedroom, where he spends most of his non-work time, sitting in front of the computer.

His cell phone rings from the bedroom desk.

I pick it up off the charger, see Yvonne's number, and take the call.

"Hello?" I say, Tommy's voice a bit raspy.

"Where the hell have you been?"

Uh-oh. She's pissed.

"Sick," is all I can say.

"Listen, I know you're taking this hard, but I need to know if I can count on you."

I have no idea what she's talking about. "Count on me for what?"

"To finish the Bova Holdings story. You've been AWOL since Lara died, and we need this story *before* the council votes on the land use change next week. If you can't do it, let me know, and I'll finish it, but I need your notes, your interviews, everything."

"When do you need it?"

"Tonight? I know the funeral is tomorrow, and I don't think any of us will be in shape to do much of anything then. But maybe we can finish it together at the office? Are you up for an all-nighter? Katelynn has already offered to help if needed."

Hearing about Lara's funeral makes my stomach feel sicker than it already was. Somehow, I manage to hold down whatever I didn't puke up earlier.

"Well?" Yvonne asks.

I stare at Tommy's desk and his locked computer. I

have no idea where to start, but can't say no to Yvonne. This sounds like a huge story, and I can't let Tommy drop the ball, even if he was ready to check out just hours ago.

"Yeah, just give me some time to clean up."

"Too late, I'm at your front door."

Shit!

"Okay," I say into the phone, then hang up.

I go to the door and open it.

It's weird seeing a host after I've been in it. I feel almost like she should recognize me or something. *Hey, you used to be me!* But she doesn't seem to sense anything weird.

"How are you?" She closes the door behind her then comes over to hug me.

"Okay," I say, struggling to keep my emotions, Tommy's emotions, in check.

She looks down at the trash bags lined up along the kitchen bar. The bags are white, and she can see the outlines of many beer bottles. I see her looking at them, but she doesn't say anything.

Instead she says, "So, you want to do this here or back at the office?"

I don't know how to tell her that I can't even log into the computer, let alone remember anything about the story. I can't tell her the truth. *Can I?* She might have her own missing memories from the day I was in her. Maybe she can be the person I open up to and tell what's going on.

"Back at the office," I say, hoping that'll give Tommy's brain time to inform me.

I go into my bedroom, look at all the folders, spiral notebooks, and papers littering Tommy's desk, clueless as to which ones might be relevant to the story. I see a flash drive in the computer. Assuming it has his latest work, I grab it and put it in my shirt pocket. I spot a leather satchel filled with my laptop, notebooks, and papers. I take it.

What about all these other papers?

I find a backpack in the small closet and stuff all the papers on his desk into it.

I head back to the living room with the satchel and the backpack.

Yvonne looks at me funny. "I didn't know we were going camping."

I laugh.

We drive to the office in separate cars, which gives Tommy's brain time to come back online and fill me in on some basics.

He's working on an investigative piece about how the developer Bova Holdings is seeking a land use change so they can build some high-priced condos on land designated for single family homes and parks. It seems like standard stuff that interests few people outside of local environmentalists. The story gets interesting once you piece together some of Bova's behind-the-scenes activities, including the fact that the company, or its subsidiaries, have given cushy jobs to friends and family of Councilman Gray, Councilwoman Hollingsworth, and Mayor Samuels. Tommy's also tracked campaign donations from people associated with Bova Holdings to the same council members.

There are still calls to make, people we need to corroborate what we have from sources we can't name, and some other miscellaneous work before the story can go to print.

I'm not sure how useful I'll be, but now that the drugs and alcohol are wearing off, I hope Tommy's memories will keep helping me piece the story together. Plus, Yvonne has been working with Tommy chasing down a lot of the leads.

I arrive at the office, and Tommy gives me the password I need to access his computer. As I read through his notes and parts of the story he's written so far, I'm impressed by his skills to track shit down.

As I'm printing stuff for Yvonne and Katelynn to read over, I find a note with a name that hits me like a hammer — Pastor James Wilson of the First Baptist Church — the pastor on the flash drive that Vinnie gave to Councilman Gray.

Wilson's church sits on a piece of land that Bova's has been trying to buy. The developer, Peter Bova, tried to get the city to declare eminent domain on the property to seize it from the church, but there were too many hoops to jump through, and it could draw too much attention to the project, which Bova is trying to avoid.

This explains why Gray wanted the drive. Leverage against Wilson, to force him to sell and avoid the other course of action.

Pastor Wilson also happens to be one of Tommy's sources in the allegations against Bova Holdings. Wilson supplied many of the documents that spurred the *Chronicle's* investigation into what seemed, on the surface, like ordinary business. And while in Vinnie's body, I helped screw Wilson by giving that drive to Councilman Gray. This makes me wish I'd watched what was on there, to see exactly what they had on Wilson. Was it a minor indiscretion, like getting a lap dance? Or did they catch him doing something illegal — drugs, prostitutes, or something else that wouldn't just ruin his standing in the community, but land him in jail?

After a few hours spent digging through public records, I find more connections between Bova Holdings and the three city council members, mostly in the form of past campaign contributions given by shell companies or individuals, so as to avoid the $950 individual and other entity caps. It's all black and white once the dots are connected, which surprises me. The developer and council members either didn't think anyone would put two and two together, or didn't care if they did. Judging from conversations in the newsroom, it seems that the city council, and developers, feel they have carte blanche to do as they please, knowing the *Daily* won't take them to task. It seems that the paper is heavily influenced by advertisers loyal to Bova Holdings, and it doesn't want to rock the boat and capsize their funding.

Mix advertising with editorial, and you defang the power of the press. You get collusion. You have uninformed voters who don't even realize that their government is ceding to the will of Big Business. I can tell that Tommy gets a great sense of pride in working for a smaller press that can still accomplish good in the community. I wonder which advertisers the *Chronicle* has to please in order to keep *its* funding. Is the *Chronicle* truly fighting the good fight, or is it embroiled in a proxy war between rival business interests?

Just thinking about it all makes me ill, but I keep pouring through the documents, adding finishing touches to the story.

My phone rings just before lunch.

Private Number.

I pick up the phone. "Hello?"

A man's voice: "Mr. Clarke?"

"Yes."

"It's Pastor Wilson. Do you have time to meet with me?"

"I'm kind of in the middle of something."

"It's about the story you're working on. We need to talk."

"We can't do it over the phone?"

"No. I need to see you, and your editor, if possible."

"Okay, hold on a second."

I tell Yvonne what's happening, and we agree to meet the pastor behind our paper's small shopping center.

❧

FIFTEEN MINUTES LATER, Yvonne and I are standing outside at a picnic table and bench behind the *Chronicle* where staffers often sit and either shoot the shit or hash out stories. Dark clouds and a cool breeze promise rain.

As we wait, Yvonne sighs. "I'm sorry that we've gotta come back here after the service. I know none of us will feel like doing shit after that."

"Maybe it's better this way," I say. "Being alone the past few days didn't do much for me. But being back here, working on something that matters, it's helping."

"Yeah, I'm the same way." Yvonne nods, looking like she wants to say something more but unsure how to bring it up. Finally, she just comes out with it, as she's prone to doing.

"Are you blaming yourself … for not asking her out when you could have? Thinking maybe she might not have been looking to meet someone online if you two were together?"

I hadn't been thinking that, but I'm sure Tommy must have been. That would help explain his overwhelming guilt.

I nod.

"Why didn't you ask her out? You know she thought the world of you."

"Are you trying to make me cry?" I ask, half joking and the rest of me serious. "You think I don't feel bad?"

"I'm sorry, I just never quite understood why you two

didn't get together. I know, I know, it's not my business, and as your boss, I probably shouldn't even have condoned such relationships in the office. It's just … I dunno. So fucking sad."

"I know." I'm fighting the urge to fall into Tommy's wallowing depression. In addition to his feelings, I now have *Lara's regret* for not getting with Tommy.

We stare out in silence for a bit.

Suddenly, a heavyset man in a Seahawks baseball cap, blue jeans, a red T-shirt, and brown jacket approaches from the other direction. He's on foot. Pastor James Wilson.

"Hi," he says, waving nervously as he approaches.

I'm not sure if he's met Yvonne before, but I go ahead and introduce them, anyway.

"Mr. Wilson, this is Yvonne Lopez, the *Chronicle's* editor. Ms. Lopez, this is Pastor James Wilson of the First Baptist Church."

They shake hands and trade hellos.

Wilson doesn't just look nervous; he looks outright terrified. Councilman Gray must've threatened him.

So, why is he here?

Yvonne asks, "So what did you want to talk to us about?"

"I need you to cancel the story."

"What?" I shout.

"I need you to cancel the story. I've decided to sell the land. Bova Holdings made me a very generous offer, and I've decided to take it."

"Wait a second," Yvonne says, before I can talk, "what happened to 'The only way they'll get this land from me is to claw it from my cold, dead hands?'"

"I've had a change of heart," he says, looking down.

"Bullshit," I say, "they got to you."

The pastor looks up at me, eyes wide, shaking his head. "I had a change of heart is all. It's difficult enough to lead the congregation under normal circumstances, but a lot of people in town work for Bova Holdings and many of them go to my church. Do you understand how much a prolonged legal battle would damage our congregation?"

"You knew this when you came to the *Chronicle*, begging us to look into Bova Holdings. You were prepared for a fight. Something's changed." I press him. "What do they have on you?"

Yvonne looks at me. Her grin says she's proud of me for calling him on his bullshit.

"Have on me?" His face is turning red, and I'm surely pushing my luck. I don't care.

"Yes, have on you. I know how these people operate. They've done something to force your hand. I want to know what that is."

He ignores my question and turns to Yvonne.

"If you run this article, you're going to destroy whatever peace we've reached. You'll risk the sale of our church — they're offering us more than enough money to rebuild, in a better location. And you'll destroy our congregation. I'm begging you, please don't run this article."

I want to say no, screw that, but I let my boss talk.

"I'm sorry, Mr. Wilson, this story isn't just about you and the church, it's about an abuse of public trust, possible illegal dealings, and now, maybe extortion. I can't kill a story because you're scared."

Wilson's face turns redder. His brows furrow and his voice becomes sharp, threatening. "If you run this story, I will disavow anything attributed to me."

"We have you on tape," I say.

He glares at me. "I'll say it's edited, taken out of context, something."

Yvonne says, "So, you'll lie?"

"I don't want to lie, but I will do whatever it takes to protect my church."

We're at a standoff.

I want to tell him I know about the flash drive, but I have no idea what kind of fallout there'll be, or what risk I might be putting Tommy and the paper in. These people don't screw around, and while Tommy and Yvonne might be willing to go full court press on Bova Holdings and the council members, they *do not* want to tangle with Mr. Bruno and his associates.

I keep my mouth shut.

Pastor Wilson gives it a final attempt, putting on his kindest smile as if he wasn't threatening us with fire and brimstone just seconds ago. "Please, I'm begging you. Think of what you'll do to my church, to this community. Please, reconsider."

Yvonne says, "We'll think about it, Pastor."

"Thank you." He shakes our hands then walks back toward wherever he parked.

"So, are you going to kill the story?" I ask once he's gone.

"Hell no," Yvonne says, smiling.

"Would it be wrong for me to ask you to marry me?" I joke.

She laughs then leads us back inside.

AFTER LUNCH, Katelynn has an assignment to cover, leaving Yvonne and me alone in the newsroom to work on the story. There are other people in the office, but they're up front, and we're sitting next to one another at a large four-person desk, out of earshot.

I want to capitalize on our moment alone and try to find out if Yvonne has any recollection of her missing day. I've never had a chance to talk to someone whose body I've been in before. I think I have an avenue without giving myself away.

"I'm sorry for not coming in the past few days."

"It's okay," she says. "I understand."

"No, it was selfish of me. I was so wrapped up in my own pain that I didn't consider that the paper had to go on and that you all were working. I don't know how you did it, and I hope I can make it up to you, leaving you all like that."

"It's okay. We all handle grief differently. And while Lara was like a sister to me, I know you had a close relationship with her, too."

"It's so weird. I don't even feel like I was myself the past few days. It's like I wasn't here, or as if someone else took over while I was off grieving. Do you know what I mean?"

I look at her, seeing a sense of recognition, and feel hopeful.

"I was feeling like that on Sunday. Felt like I was walking around in a daze. Barely remember a thing."

"But you do remember some things?"

"Yeah, I remember things that happened, but it's kind of foggy, like I was drunk or something."

"Yeah," I agree, so she doesn't wonder too much about her own memories. "Same here."

Not for the first time, I'm wondering how this all works. When I'm in someone, are the hosts still there, witnessing events as if *they're* experiencing them? Or do they wake up the next day with their memories filling the gaps once I'm gone, giving them the relevant information they need while filtering out my involvement?

Memory isn't some unchanging hardware engraved into the brain's circuitry. It's more like pliable software, restructuring itself each time it's processed or called upon. This is something I've researched over the past year as I try and recover my memories from the life before this. Memories aren't static events. They're merely interpretations. Meaning and understanding can change wildly depending on many factors. It makes perfect sense that the host's brain would deceive them, sort of how your brain attempts to make sense of weird dreams. The host's brain tries to illuminate something that shouldn't make sense. As if the brain is programmed to keep things logical and in order — a coping mechanism to prevent the person from going mad.

I ask a few more questions, keeping them broad so I don't attract too much attention, but pointed enough to maybe gain a grasp of what's happening.

I feel a sense of accomplishment, for the first time in years. While this is only a theory, it helps me to figure this out a bit more. I also feel a little less guilty for the significant events I've robbed from people — first kisses, a child's first steps, achieving an important victory at work. It would seem that the hosts, based on Yvonne's comments, at least, do remember their lost days.

Yvonne changes the subject after a while, asking, "So, what kind of dirt do you think Bova has on Pastor Williams?"

"I dunno, but that's the only thing that makes sense, right?"

"Maybe they sent someone to threaten the pastor?"

"Does Bova work with people like that?"

Yvonne laughs. "Does a bear shit in the woods?"

I'm quiet for a moment, then ask, "So why are we

writing this story? Aren't you worried they might come after you, or the paper?"

"Let them try. I'll show those *cabrones* they can't intimidate me."

"*Cabrones?*"

"Motherfuckers," she says, smiling.

"Yvonne, you are one tough *cabrona*," I say, grinning like an idiot who just learned his first Spanish curse word.

WE WORK THROUGH DINNERTIME.

As I'm putting the finishing touches on the story, Yvonne is on the phone with Detective Ramirez, trying to find out if there's been any word on Allie.

This reminds me of something I'd almost forgotten — Madam Monique. I look up her number, put it into my phone, and wait for a free moment when I can go outside and make the call. I'm not sure what I'll say, or if I'll even get a hold of her, but I have to try.

I finish what I hope will be the story's final edit, print it out, and hand it to Yvonne. As she looks over my copy, I cut outside.

I call Madam Monique's line and wait for an answer.

It cuts to voice mail.

I hang up.

I stand behind the *Chronicle*, pacing, wondering how long I should wait before calling back.

I make it five minutes.

Voicemail again.

I decide to leave a message. "Hello, this is Thomas Clarke of the *Bay Cove Chronicle*. We're doing a feature piece on the best psychics on the West Coast, and we'd love to interview Madam Monique for our story."

I leave a number to reach me and hope she calls tonight.

I head back into the office.

Yvonne is standing up, my story in her hand, "Brav-Fucking-O, sir! You nailed those bastards! It's clear, concise, and explains to our readers why they need to care. Easily the best story we've ever run."

"Really?" I must be blushing.

"You're the real deal, Tommy. I have no doubt that I'm going to be seeing you on *60 Minutes* someday, tearing the asshole out of some lying politician."

"Thank you." I sit down, a smile pushing my cheeks up high enough to hurt. I'm happy for Tommy, and Yvonne. They needed something good this week.

"We're gonna piss a lot of people off," I warn.

"Good, we need to stir shit up, and wake up the voters before this nonsense goes to council."

I can tell that Yvonne is up for the fight. And while Tommy might have lost some steam following Lara's death, Yvonne is using the tragedy to fuel her. She can't do anything to bring her friend back or do much to find Allie, but she can battle the enemies she can see, and damn it if she'd let anyone stop her.

"Want to help me find some photos for the story?"

Usually, this would be the graphic designer's job, but since Yvonne hasn't replaced her yet, the task falls to us.

"Yeah." I roll my chair next to hers as she searches our archives for photos of the council members and Peter Bova.

The faces are all familiar to me through Tommy's memories. As I look at them it's like seeing pictures of people I've only heard described in stories, maybe seen illustrations of. In person, they all look a bit different than Tommy's memories.

"Usually, we run head shots in stories like this, but I want these to stand out," Yvonne explains as she combs through search results with Bova, most of the results coming from candids snapped at various functions. Something jumps out as she skims.

"Go back!" I point to her screen.

"What?" Yvonne looks at me, alarmed.

She clicks back one shot.

"Not that one. Keep going."

She flips back another shot, then again.

And there, I see the impossible. It's from a black tie charity event three years ago, a bunch of well-dressed people standing together, chatting, drinks in hand. And there's Gavin, standing right beside Peter Bova.

My heart races.

It's him, but I can't say anything, not without a lot of explaining.

"Who is that man to Peter Bova's right?"

"Why?" she asks, still confused.

"He looks so familiar," I say, hoping like hell that *she* will remember him in some fashion, hoping she'll have some recognition from my memories.

She looks at a text file associated with the photo file's name.

"The man to Peter Bova's right is his son, Alexander Bova."

Her eyes widen.

"What is it?" I ask.

"I think that's him."

"Who?"

"Gavin! The man who killed Lara!"

"Are you sure?" I ask, jumping up and down inside, screaming, *Yes, yes, yes!*

"I think so," she says.

"We've got to call the detective," I urge.

She reaches for her phone.

Suddenly a voice calls out, "Put down the phone!"

We both turn, surprised that someone sneaked through the back door, and is now standing here, pointing a gun at us.

The man is wearing a black mask, but I'd know Vinnie's voice anywhere. He's here to clean up the mess.

YVONNE SLOWLY LOWERS THE PHONE.

"What do you want? We don't have money on hand."

"I know," Vinnie says. "I'm here to ask you to reconsider the story you're running."

"What story?" Yvonne asks.

"The one that Pastor Williams came to you with. You need to kill the story."

Yvonne is too pissed to take his suggestion. "Excuse me. Who the hell are you to walk in here thinking you can tell us to kill a story?"

She reaches into her desk where she keeps her gun.

Vinnie fires two shots, one to the head, one to the chest. Yvonne slumps over.

I scream, "Vinnie, no!"

Vinnie's gun is already on me. There is a moment of pause in his eyes, but his finger is already squeezing the trigger.

I hear him say, "Sorry," and then there is nothing.

Chapter Seven

FRIDAY, 5:00 a.m.

I WAKE up gasping for air, hearing the bleating alarm.

I hit the off button and sit bolt upright, flicking on the light next to the bed.

I'm in the body of Detective Hector Ramirez, alone in his bedroom. A picture of his ex-wife and twin girls is still on his nightstand, though she took the kids when she split two years ago.

They're still the first thing he sees each morning — a reminder of what he sacrificed for the job, and a mental note to never let the bullshit get to him.

Unlike waking up inside the dazed and confused Thomas and Vinnie, I feel laser focused as Hector. It's as if he's been waiting for me.

One can only hope.

I get on the phone immediately to my sergeant, asking for an update on last night's shootings. I tell him I saw something on the news, even though I've yet to turn on the TV.

"You want info on the shootings or the fire?" Sergeant Shields asks.

"Everything."

"Two gunshots, one DOA, one airlifted to Bay Cove General."

"There was a survivor? Who?"

"Yvonne Lopez, she's in critical condition. Doctors don't know if she'll make it."

I'm surprised she survived the two shots, particularly since one hit her in the head.

"What about the fire?"

"Whoever did the shooting torched the place. There's nothing left of the *Chronicle*."

"Jesus." Anger courses through me. I want to find Vinnie and arrest him. But I have more important things to do right now — chief among them, find Alexander Bova and save Allie.

I'm about to hang up when I get a flash of memory from Hector. "Who's heading the case?"

"Parker and Gillespie."

Given that those two clowns are among the estimated 30 percent of the sheriff's department, including the sheriff himself, who are either crooked or somehow involved with Mr. Bruno's criminal empire, this doesn't bode well for Yvonne's odds of survival.

And there's nothing I can say to Shields that won't put Hector in the crosshairs. My only hope is that the deputies won't do something insanely stupid, like attempting to kill Yvonne while she's still in the hospital.

"Thanks," I say to Shields, then hang up.

I take a shower, sorting through Hector's memories, searching for the best way to find Alexander Bova in a way that won't draw attention from my superiors. If I look him up in the database, there's a good chance someone will see it and then Hector will wind up with a bullet in his head, too.

First, Lara is murdered; then Allie is kidnapped. Now Vinnie's killed Tommy and sent Yvonne to the hospital.

I can't risk another life. I have to play this safe.

My anger builds as I dress.

No, I can't play it safe. I need to go on the offensive.

I get a flash of memory from Monday night, the call that Hector was first on scene for — Vinnie's club.

The money and hard drives I logged into evidence lockup until the case is closed.

I ARRIVE at the sheriff's office, make my morning rounds, then head to evidence lockup, saying I need to check on something.

I sign in, am buzzed into the evidence room, and close the door behind me. I follow Hector's memories to locate the shelf where the evidence is stored.

I find several sacks of cash in one bag, and seven hard drives, each in their own evidence bag.

But something's wrong.

As I examine one of the hard drives more closely through the clear plastic, I see something that causes my heart to sink. While the bags each have a sticker with Hector's name and signature and description of the contents, these aren't the same hard drives that Hector logged into evidence.

Someone got in here and tampered with the bags.

Fuck!

I toss the bags back onto the shelf, seething.

I want to know who did this. I want their badges. I want to see them rotting in prison.

Fuckers.

I compose myself and leave the lockup, then sign out and return to my desk. I can feel eyes on me and don't know who to rely on. There are a few people Hector trusts, but no one implicitly. The thing about corruption is that it not only erodes an institution, but it also erodes the spirit of those who try to stay above the influence of corruption as well. It's damn hard for most of the deputies on the force to turn down the perks that come with the Dark Side. From little things like extra money and over-time security assignments at posh places to accessing Sheriff Dixon's inner circle, do what *they* want, and your path is easy. But to do the right thing, to stay on the straight and narrow, is nearly impossible working under a corrupt sheriff.

Hector would be a marked man if his father hadn't been a legend on the force who died in the line of duty. That earned him respect from even the most corrupt cops on the force. It also meant they didn't ask him to join their little party or to do anything he didn't want to do.

He hoped to ride out Sheriff Dixon's administration. If he could weather the storm until the next election, he could hang onto his job, and hopefully, help weed out the bad deputies alongside whoever the next sheriff might be.

There were a few people on the force, other officers like Hector who were hungry for change. Many of them even said they'd back him if he ran for sheriff.

Naturally, Hector said he wasn't interested. If Dixon knew he was going to run, he'd make Hector's life a living hell.

So, Hector bides his time, trying to fly under the radar.

I don't know how to keep him invisible now if I'm

going to save Allie and go after Bova's son. It's impossible to believe I won't be making enemies.

I mull my options then head out in my car with an idea.

If I were Mr. Bruno, where would I hide my hard drives after my club was robbed?

I'd put them right back in the same place. It's the last thing the Russians, whoever they are, would probably expect. Hell, Mr. Bruno, or Vinnie specifically, probably took care of them already.

I decide to test my theory.

THE EMERALD CLUB, despite its reputation as a high-end gentleman's club, is located in one of the seedier parts of town along a stretch of road known mostly for its airport-adjacent abandoned storefronts, crumbling hotels, and greasy spoons.

The club is a giant pink-and-black square of a building with no windows, save for the front doors.

I drive around the back, which faces an old abandoned concrete factory and pinelands.

I get out of the patrol car, grab a duffel bag from my trunk, empty the contents, then take it with me as I head to the rear entrance.

"Hello?" I knock. "Sheriff's department."

No response.

I look around, just to make sure there's no one in sight, then kick in the door.

I step inside, gun raised, as if responding to a call.

"Hello, sheriff's department?"

The place is dark, save for dim red emergency lighting. Nobody seems to be home. I find the alarm box and enter the code to cancel the silent alarm before it starts screaming.

Then I head straight to the office, knowing that cameras are recording me as I do. I'm not sure how I'll deal with that, but I'll figure it out.

I head to Vinnie's office, knock on that door.

No response.

I kick in the door, head to the safe, and begin turning the dial, hoping they haven't changed the combination, and have returned the hard drives.

The door clicks unlocked.

I pull it open.

I see bags of cash and hard drives, just as expected.

I smile.

Finally, a win.

I grab the hard drives, *and* the cash to help Hector's family escape if things go south, then shove them into the duffel.

~

Two hours later

~

I HEAD into Sheriff Dixon's office and close the door behind me.

He looks up from his desk, surprised to see me standing there, much less having closed the door.

Dixon is a big man, six-foot-five former college line-backer with broad shoulders, a large square jaw, and a big head topped with sandy blond hair. At fifty-six, he's more gut than muscle, but he's still an intimidating man, particularly when he's about a foot and a half taller than Hector.

"Ramirez, what's going on?" He doesn't get up from his seat and barely looks up.

I set my phone down on his desk and slide it to him.

"Press play."

He does.

His brows furrow, face turning red as he watches the video of him cavorting with whores in the back of The Emerald Club.

"What the hell?" He finally stands, fists balled like he's about to knock me out, or maybe reach into my body and rip out my heart.

"There are six more like that, so I suggest you sit your ass down."

His eyes widen.

"I said sit."

He does, reluctantly.

"What do you think you're doing?"

"Don't worry, sir, I'm not looking to embarrass you. I just need a favor, and it's probably one you won't want to do, so I'm setting the stakes up for you now. That's one of the many videos on drives I stole from The Emerald Club. I have every one they had in their safe, and man, are there some disturbing things on there with some high-profile people."

He's glaring at me. "What do you want?"

"I need you to find someone."

"Who?"

"Alexander Bova."

"The developer's son?"

"One and the same," I say, smiling.

"And do what?"

"Arrest him for the murder of Lara Spencer and the kidnapping of Allie Martin."

"What? Is this a joke?"

"No, sir. And you need to find and arrest him before he kills Allie."

"How do you know he has her, or that he killed Lara Spencer? I thought it was some guy named Gavin."

"I got it from a concerned citizen, a citizen who knows this office is corrupt and won't act on the tip. So I'm making sure we do."

He stares at me. I wonder if he's going to pretend he's not corrupt, or try to explain his behavior. Maybe stand and attack me. His gears are turning, and I don't trust what they'll come up with once they stop.

"Before you answer," I add, "You need to know that if anything happens to me, or to Mrs. Lopez, copies of these hard drives will be sent to several media outlets *and* the FBI."

"Copies?"

"You heard me. Now, are you going to help me do the right thing?"

"And if I do?"

"I give you the hard drives and the copies. Your reputation remains intact. You and your crooked council members and developer friends can all keep slicing and dicing the city as you see fit."

"I want the hard drives, and the copies, first."

"This isn't a negotiation. You'll do what I ask, and then I'll deliver."

"Why are you doing this? You realize you're about to make some very powerful enemies, right?"

"I'm doing it because it's my duty to protect and serve. And right now there's a monster out there doing whatever he wants because he knows you won't stop him. Hell, I wouldn't be surprised if the department knew he was a murderer, but didn't want to rock the boat."

"That's bullshit," Dixon says.

"Well then, let's do the right thing."

~

SHERIFF DIXON GETS a location on Alex Bova and sets up a squad, of my choosing, to go in and rescue the girl.

Unfortunately, the most qualified deputies for this engagement are men I don't particularly trust, save for two. But I have no choice if I want to give Allie the best possible odds. We have a unit of six deputies, dressed all in black gear, rebreathers, and tear gas grenades, including myself.

As night is falling, we stage three blocks away from the house where Bova is staying, a rental he pays for under an assumed identity.

Sergeant Edmund, one of the two deputies I trust, is running point. We go over the plan of attack once more before driving to Bova's block, lights off, and exit four doors down from his house.

Three of the officers head to the property's rear.

I race toward the front door with a battering ram, along with Edmund and Harris. No knocks or warnings.

We burst through the door, toss the grenades, then storm the house while the remaining agents enter from the rear.

"Sheriff's department, get on the ground!" Edmund shouts, though we don't see anyone through the smoke.

Shotgun ready, I frantically search for the basement door.

It's not in the kitchen, nor the living room, the most obvious of spots.

"Help me find a hidden door to the basement!" I shout.

Seconds later, one of the deputies calls over the radio, "Found it, behind a bookcase in one of the bedrooms."

I race to join them as they pull the bookcase aside.

I'm about to enter the room when an explosion rips through the team. A hot blast slams me back into the hallway, hitting the wall behind me, hard.

Fucking booby trap!

A high-pitched piercing screams into my ears and kills every other sound.

I can't see anything but black smoke and quickly spreading flames.

"Does anyone copy?" I know I'm yelling but can't hear my voice. "Anyone?"

Nothing.

Shit.

There's movement in the darkness, a dark figure in front of the flames. Gavin … no, Alexander Bova, standing there with a shotgun aimed at a downed deputy.

He fires.

I don't think he's spotted me in the hall yet. He steps toward another of the fallen officers and aims his weapon.

I reach for mine, only to discover that it's still in the room — dropped when the blast knocked me back.

My hands scramble for the knife tucked into a sheath on my belt. I grab it then launch myself up and into the room.

Bova turns just as I'm about to close in on him.

He levels his gun at me.

I scream, reaching out, thrusting the shotgun's barrel up as he fires.

The gun booms in his hand; buckshot hits the ceiling.

Bova tries to wrench the gun away from me, but I drag the blade down and over his left hand, slicing through his white-knuckle grip.

He screams, dropping the gun.

I thrust the knife into his gut, then drive it straight up for maximum damage.

His wide eyes meet mine.

"You!" he growls.

I'm not sure if he recognizes *me* in yet another body, nor do I care any longer. I just want him dead.

I withdraw the blade then shove it up through his neck.

He slumps to the ground, my blade still in him.

Fire is now licking the walls around me. Black smoke fills the room.

I grab a rebreather off one of the fallen deputies then run through the exploded doorway and down the concrete stairs, glad they're still intact.

Allie is lying face down on the ground, blood pooling around her.

"No!" I scream.

He fucking killed her when he heard us coming.

No! No! No! I can't let her die. I can't!

I run to Allie and flip her over.

Her eyes open, unfocused, dark, but she's still alive. I slip the rebreather onto her so she won't inhale the smoke then scoop her up and carry her up the stairs.

The fire is raging.

I can barely see an aperture of darkness among the flames. I rush through, praying not to trip.

I make it out of the bedroom and into the living room where Deputy Edmund is standing, gun drawn on me.

He stares at me.

Maybe I misjudged my hand, or maybe Sheriff Dixon didn't care what got out, as it wasn't as bad as the wrath of Mr. Bruno and Peter Bova.

Dixon told Edmund to kill me, to clean every loose end.

Edmund lowers his gun, and I realize I was wrong. He must've thought I was Bova, trying to escape.

"Come on," he says.

I follow him out into the cold night air.

❧

DAY 363

❧

I'M SITTING in the hospital room, struggling to stay awake, to stay in this body.

I've never been able to stay up much longer than twenty-six hours before passing out and jumping bodies.

We're on hour twenty-nine now.

I need to stay awake long enough to see Yvonne come out of this.

I've been passing the time reading to her and telling her what happened, hoping there's some part of her in there that can hear me.

I have a feeling there is.

❧

HER EYES OPEN AT NOON.

I feel tears as she speaks. "Detective Ramirez?"

I want to tell her *No, it's me, the person who'd been inside Lara, Tommy, Allie, and her. It's me, your friend without a name, without his or her own body.*

And at that moment, I'm torn between great joy that she's alive and tremendous sorrow that I, the real me, can't share this happiness with her.

A doctor comes in and asks me to step out for a bit so he can check Yvonne's stats.

After nearly a half hour, a nurse says I can go back.

This time, I've brought a visitor.

YVONNE BURSTS into tears as she sees who I'm pushing in the wheelchair.

"Allie! You're alive!"

"Yeah, more or less," Allie says.

"She lost a lot of blood, but her injuries weren't too bad," I explain.

"I'm so happy to see you," Yvonne says, overwhelmed with joy. She reaches her hand out, and the two girls lock fingers.

I want to hug them both, let them know I'm here with them, that we got through this together, but I'm more or less a stranger.

Allie looks back at me and says, "Detective Ramirez saved me and killed that fucker who murdered Lara."

Yvonne looks at me, her eyes wet. "Thank you."

I nod. "You're both very welcome."

Another nurse comes in and says, "Allie, your mother is here to see you."

I allow the nurse to wheel Allie out. As they reach the door, Allie looks up at us and says, "Bye."

We wave goodbye.

Now that we're alone, I go to Yvonne's bedside and explain everything that happened at the *Chronicle*, how Tommy died, and that someone burned the place down.

She breaks down again, and I feel terrible delivering this news to her after she's just woken up. But I don't know how much longer I have before I fall asleep.

"I also want you to know that you're going to be safe now."

She looks up at me. "How do you know that?"

"Because of this." I hold up the flash drive.

"What's that?"

"Maybe a Pulitzer for you," I say. "Justice for Tommy? The end of a corrupt era here? Everything you need to bring this damned circus down."

"How am I gonna do that? I don't have an office."

"You won't need an office. I've found an investigative reporter who will help you bring these fuckers down."

She stares at me like she's not sure if I can be trusted.

"Why are you doing this?"

"Because it's the right thing to do."

"Thank you." She reaches out to hold my hand.

"No, thank *you*," I say. "It's people like you who make this all worth fighting for."

I TELL her goodbye and head to the bus station with my bag of cash. Also in the bag, a note telling Hector to watch the video I recorded on a burner phone. A video that will explain everything and tell him how to protect his family from the shit storm that will hit when Yvonne's article goes national.

As I lean against the window of the bus, watching fields of greenery pass in a gentle flow, I see a smile creep across Hector's face.

For the first time in a long time, I feel like I've actually made a difference.

Epilogue

DAY 368

∾

Los Orillas, California

∾

Today I'm in the body of fitness instructor Steph Wimberly. She's twenty-six and beautiful, the daughter of an entertainment mogul, living like most people can only dream.

Life inside her body feels like a vacation.

But the best part is that she lives in Los Orillas, California, and I have a chance to go back and see the psychic, maybe get some answers.

My memories of Lara, Allie, and the others are surprisingly still with me, which is good because I've been able to track what's happening in Bay Cove on the news.

After I left, the Associated Press printed a story with

Yvonne and the other reporter detailing the city's deeply entrenched system of corruption.

The story went national, with the feds stepping in to arrest and replace the sheriff, along with three of the five council members. Bova Holdings was in a tailspin, and Peter Bova has fled the country following allegations of his involvement, and revelations of what his son had been up to.

Vinnie Fortunato was found dead in his house, in bed with two women — his girlfriend and an exotic dancer. Foul play is suspected.

While several stories have also surfaced regarding Mr. Bruno, none have identified the man or found a photo. He has since vanished, with the prevailing wisdom that he was living under a false identity and is now doing the same somewhere else. Perhaps he is starting a new criminal organization.

I PULL up in Madam Monique's parking lot.

I leave the car and head inside.

Staci greets me with a smile, the kind reserved for people like Steph Wimberly.

"Hi, and welcome to Madam Monique's, do you have an appointment?"

"No," I say, "I'm very sorry, but this is a last-minute emergency."

I pull out my purse, fumble through wads of cash and credit cards, including her black AmEx, which will turn any merchant into her best friend. I raise my nose, just a bit, to adopt the I'm-better-than-you vibe that always gets Steph what she wants.

"Listen, I'll pay whatever it takes. I just need a few minutes."

"Hold on a second."

Staci heads through the door into Madam's back room, then returns a moment later.

"Madam will see you now."

I hand her my AmEx then pass through the door.

When I enter the room, the old woman has her eyes closed, just like last time when I was here as Charles. The names might change; the show stays the same.

Madam invites me to sit across from her.

I do.

I wait for her to open her eyes.

She asks for my hands.

I reach across the table to take her hands, expecting some sort of spark.

Nothing.

Hmm …

She mumbles her prayer or whatever it is, then opens her eyes.

I meet her gaze, hoping she'll see me inside this blonde heiress. But then something occurs to me.

There's something different in *her* eyes.

I decide to speak. "I just want to thank you for seeing me on such short notice."

"You're welcome, dear," she says.

"You come so highly recommended. Two of my friends come to you and couldn't speak higher praises of you."

"Oh, really? Who?"

"Danny Shar and Charles Tompkins."

I wait for a reaction.

But her expression never changes, nor is there any recognition of the *me* inside this blonde shell.

Madam Monique is smiling. "Oh, they're such sweet gentlemen. How do you know them?"

"We go to the same gym," I lie.

"Oh. So, what would you like today? Your fortune told? A palm reading? Perhaps a seance with a dearly departed?"

"My palm read," I say, and offer my hand.

"Certainly."

She does her little prayer whispering routine before she gets on with the show. I listen, trying to pick up on any recognizable words, or language. I don't think she's speaking in tongues, but it sounds like gibberish to me.

She finally takes my hand.

She is feeling my skin, talking nonsense about refinement, energy, and the flexibility of my mind. Then she starts on some silly stuff about archetypes, and a sudden realization washes over me.

I'm not sure how I know it, but I feel an unshakeable certainty.

She isn't the same woman who read my palm!

"You aren't her, are you?" I ask, surprised as the words leave my mouth.

"Aren't who?"

A part of me wants to recant, explain it away as something else. But I feel so close to discovery — of what I don't yet know — that I push forward instead.

"You don't remember me, do you?"

She looks up at me with a vague, confused smile, as if I'm asking a trick question to ferret out the truth, to expose her ruse. She says, "I'm sorry, what?" likely not wanting to give a yes or no response which would back her into a corner.

"I came in here before, except I wasn't me. I was in someone else's body." I feel a tremendous relief, finally speaking the truth, and danger, knowing I could harm my host if things get out of hand. What if Madam calls the police, says this crazy woman came in talking about being in another body? I need to be cautious, but it's hard when I feel so close to something.

Madam takes her hand from mine, eyeing me nervously as if she's considering calling for Staci.

"It's okay," I say as calmly as I can. "I'm not crazy. But please, hear me out, will you? You might be the only person who can help me."

I don't believe in psychics or fortune tellers, but I can't believe they're all corrupt scammers looking to separate you from your money. *Some* must truly think they have powers. Maybe those people are tapping into something we can't understand, even if it's not what they believe it to be. And if that's the case, maybe I can appeal to the part of her that wants to help. Maybe she'll remember someone else being in her body, or meeting me when I came in as Charles.

Maybe.

Her eyes are wary, but she seems receptive to hearing me out.

"Madam Monique, do you remember anything weird happening last Wednesday? Like maybe you weren't quite yourself?"

I don't want to say too much or lead the witness.

Her eyes suddenly lock onto mine. Confusion has turned to something between fear and recognition.

She does remember — *something.*

"H-How do you know?"

"What is it?"

"How do you know?" she repeats. Her chair scrapes back against the floor, but she's not yet standing or bolting from the room.

I lean back in my chair to give her some space.

"I'll tell you, but first you have to tell me what you remember, just to make sure I'm on the right path."

"I … I've always had a strong memory. I may be old, but I can remember what I had for breakfast every day back to 1951. You name a date and I can tell you the weekday it fell upon. I can remember the weather, too. A very strong memory. But Wednesday is a blur. I don't remember much. I remember meeting a few of my clients, but the oddest thing is, I can't remember what I was thinking when I met them. And I can't remember other details, like what I had for breakfast, or what show I watched before bed."

My heart races as she confirms my suspicion. Someone else was in her. There is at least one other person like me, one other Jumper.

I ask if she remembers being upset during any of her readings.

"Yes, though I can't remember why. It's the weirdest thing. And I've since called the client to apologize, and ya wanna hear something even weirder?"

I nod.

"He doesn't remember, either. He remembers some of it, just like me, but not the finer details."

I confess: "It's because I was in him."

She looks at me like I admitted to being the devil.

"Well, not me, in this body you see here."

I explain, as best and succinctly as I can, what is happening to me.

Suddenly, she stands.

I'm afraid she's going to run out of the room, and the conversation is over.

But she doesn't leave.

Instead, she goes to a shelf behind her, removes a

small black wooden box painted with ornate vines and flowers and eyes. She opens the box and pulls out an envelope.

"I think this is for you." Her hand shakes with the offer. "I woke up, and this was on my bedside table. It's in my writing, but again, I don't remember writing it. I didn't know what it meant, and thought I might be losing my mind."

I take the envelope, which is tucked closed, rather than sealed.

I pull out a letter with tiny handwriting:

≈

ELLA,
   Stop searching.
   You won't like what you find.
   Better to forget and let go.
   Only then can you live again.
   — Another Traveler.

≈

I STARE AT THE LETTER, a million emotions tearing through me at once.

Tears roll down my cheeks.

I'm not alone.

Yet this other traveler is telling me to forget. To stop searching.

Why?

What does this man or woman know?

What are they warning me away from?

I don't know. It's all so overwhelming.

But now I have somewhere to start.

If the letter was meant to scare me, it's done the opposite.

For the first time in a year, I feel validation. That this isn't something I'm stuck in forever. There are answers out there, and I can find them.

I may be lost and adrift, but now I have an anchor to moor into the randomness of my wanderer's life. I have an identity to hold close.

And a name: *Ella.*

Suddenly, the number of days doesn't matter as much as this: I am not alone.

The story continues...

If you enjoyed reading *Jumper* and want to read more, the story continues in Karma Police, Book Two in the Karma Police series.

Get Karma Police Today

A Quick Favor...

If you enjoyed this book, please write a short review on your favorite online bookselling site so other readers can enjoy it, too.

Thanks so much!

About the Authors

Sean Platt is an entrepreneur and founder of Sterling & Stone, where he makes stories with his partners, Johnny B. Truant, and David W. Wright, and a family of storytellers.

Sean is the bestselling author of over 10 million words' worth of books, including the Yesterday's Gone and Invasion series. Sean is also co-author of the indie publishing cornerstone, Write. Publish. Repeat. and co-host of the Story Studio Podcast.

Originally from Long Beach, California, Sean now lives in Austin, Texas with his wife and two children. He has more than his share of nose.

David W. Wright is the co-author of edge-of-your seat thrillers including the best-selling post-apocalyptic series *Yesterday's Gone,* the paranoid sci-fi *WhiteSpace* series, and the vigilante series, *No Justice*, as well as standalone thrillers *12*, and *Crash* which was recently optioned for a movie.

David is an accomplished, though intermittent, cartoonist who lives in [LOCATION REDACTED] with his wife and son [NAMES REDACTED.]

He is not at all paranoid.

He is "the grumpy one" on the *The Story Studio Podcast* with fellow Sterling and Stone founders, Sean Platt and Johnny B. Truant.

David writes about books, TV shows, movies, and

video games he enjoys; his struggles with anxiety and OCD; writing; and posts the occasional drawing at his personal blog at davidwwright.com

You can email him at david@sterlingandstone.net

We swear, he almost never bites. Unless you feed him after midnight.

For a full list of his most recent books visit sterlingandstone.net.

Also By Sean Platt

The Dead World Series

Dead Zero

Dead City

Dead Nation

Dead Planet

Empty Nest

The Beam Series

The Beam Season One

The Beam Season Two

The Beam Season Three

Robot Proletariat Series

En3my

Robot Proletariat

The Infinite Loop

The Hard Reset

Cascade Failure

Reboot

The Tomorrow Gene Series

Null Identity

The Tomorrow Gene

The Tomorrow Clone

The Eden Experiment

Karma Police Series

Jumper

Karma Police

The Collectors

Deviant

The Fall

Homecoming

Yesterday's Gone

October's Gone

Yesterday's Gone Season One

Yesterday's Gone Season Two

Yesterday's Gone Season Three

Yesterday's Gone Season Four

Yesterday's Gone Season Five

Yesterday's Gone Season Six

Tomorrow's Gone

Tomorrow's Gone Season One

Tomorrow's Gone Season Two

Tomorrow's Gone Season Three

Available Darkness

Darkness Itself

Available Darkness Book One

Available Darkness Book Two

Available Darkness Book Three

WhiteSpace

WhiteSpace Season One

WhiteSpace Season Two

WhiteSpace Season Three

Stand Alone Novels

Burnout

The Island

Crash

Emily's List

Pattern Black

Devil May Care

The Secret Within

Also By David W. Wright

Cold Vengeance

Cold Vengeance

Cold Reckoning

Hidden Justice

Hidden Justice

Hidden Honor

Hidden Shame

Hidden Virtue

No Justice

No Justice

No Escape

No Hope

No Return

No Stopping

No Fear

Karma Police

Jumper

Karma Police

The Collectors

Deviant

The Fall

Homecoming

Yesterday's Gone

October's Gone

Yesterday's Gone Season One

Yesterday's Gone Season Two

Yesterday's Gone Season Three

Yesterday's Gone Season Four

Yesterday's Gone Season Five

Yesterday's Gone Season Six

Tomorrow's Gone

Tomorrow's Gone Season One

Tomorrow's Gone Season Two

Tomorrow's Gone Season Three

Available Darkness

Darkness Itself

Available Darkness Book One

Available Darkness Book Two

Available Darkness Book Three

WhiteSpace

WhiteSpace Season One

WhiteSpace Season Two

WhiteSpace Season Three

Stand Alone Novels

Crash

Emily's List

Threshold

The Secret Within